Tom Gates is ABSOLUTELY FANTASTIC

(at some things)

By Liz Pichon

CANDLEWICK PRESS

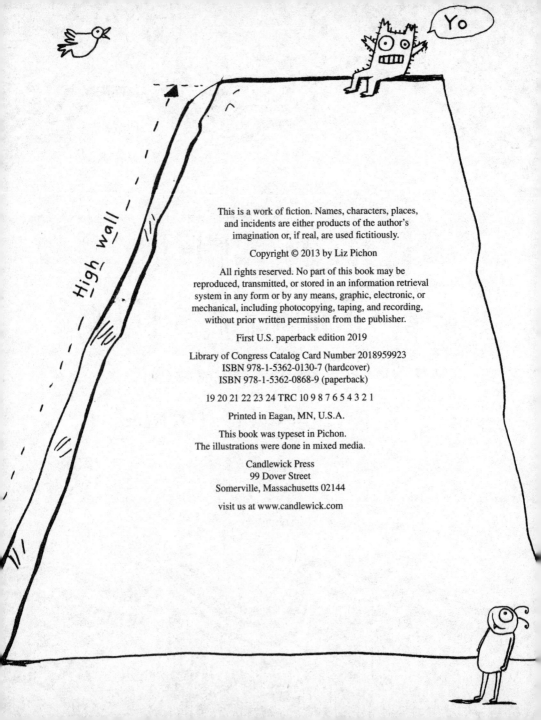

Copyright © 2013 by Liz Pichon

First U.S. paperback edition 2019

Library of Congress Catalog Card Number 2018959923
ISBN 978-1-5362-0130-7 (hardcover)
ISBN 978-1-5362-0868-9 (paperback)

19 20 21 22 23 24 TRC 10 9 8 7 6 5 4 3 2 1

Printed in Eagan, MN, U.S.A.

This book was typeset in Pichon.
The illustrations were done in mixed media.

Candlewick Press
99 Dover Street
Somerville, Massachusetts 02144

visit us at www.candlewick.com

High wall

Yo

For my lovely mum,
Joan,
from your
(not always so)
lovely daughter
Liz xx
        xxx

Remember
Bug-Eyed
Bear?
I still have him — he
looks like Mr. Fullerman.

EVERYWHERE!

IN THE BOOK

I WISH school started at eleven o'clock in the morning and

NOT at quarter to nine

Groan

(which is far too early for me).

I'm RUBBISH at getting up on time.

It takes me **AGES** to get my brain working, and even longer for my 👁 👁 eyes to 😐 open.

Mr. Fullerman (my teacher) is
ALWAYS WIDE-AWAKE.

Right now he's at the front of the class, being all **BUSY** and LIVELY while writing r𝖺nd𝗈m words on the board that don't make any sense at all.

He says,

"You're probably wondering why I'm writing all these words down."

(Er, slightly.)

"Does anyone want to ADD their own interesting word to this list?"

(I keep quiet.)

Then someone at the back of the classroom says, CAKE, sir. Which is a good choice (everyone likes cake, don't they?).

Mr. Fullerman writes "CAKE" on the board.

Then Mark Clump suggests BUG and Julia Morton wants PENCIL (which is NOT that interesting, but Mr. Fullerman writes it down anyway). ALL the time I'm thinking to myself — I wonder WHY Mr. Fullerman never ever seems to look tired?

MAYBE it's because his EYES are so MASSIVE and WIDE and STAREY? ◉ ◉

Mr. Fullerman really does have the

MOST ENORMOUS BIG BEADY EYES.

That's what I'm thinking.

Only I'm <u>NOT</u> thinking it.

I'm actually SAYING IT—

OUT-LOUD.

"BIG BEADY EYES."

"I'm sorry, Tom, did you say something?"

Mr. Fullerman is staring right at me.

 "No, sir."

"It sounded like you said BIG BEADY EYES, Tom?"

 (Think ... think ...) "No, sir."

"What was it you said, then?"

 "I said ... BIG MEATY PIES, sir."

Which makes everyone in the class LAUGH Ha! Ha! Ha!

(apart from me).

M̶r. Fullerman gives me another LOOK

and says,

"That's THREE words, Tom — choose one. "

I PANIC and say ➡ PIES,

which he writes down on the board.

M̶r. Fullerman explains what he wants us to

do next.

"I'd like you all to write a short story that includes as MANY of these WORDS on the board as you can."

"Your story can be about anything you want. So get creative!"

Great ...if I'd known THAT, I would have picked a slightly more useful word to use in a story, like IT or AND.

Definitely not PIES.

Once upon a ~~PIE~~.

~~There was a BIG PIE.~~

LIST OF WORDS

STORMY

GIGANTIC

RUNNING

SURPRISED

CAKE

NICE

SMALL

BUG

PENCIL

FRIDGE

PIES

(Mr. Fullerman didn't say the story had to make any sense, which is just as well, really — here goes.)

ENGLISH

MY SHORT STORY By Tom Gates

It was a STORMY night when I SURPRISED my grumpy sister, Delia, by RUNNING her a GIGANTIC bath. She was very happy until I pointed out there was a BUG sitting on her head. I suggested she could wash it off in the bath. But Delia got cross and tried to *flick* it away with a PENCIL instead.

Eventually when she went off to take her bath, I helped myself to the delicious PIES that were in the FRIDGE. There was CAKE too. I ate most of it. But because I am a NICE brother, I left Delia a really SMALL piece. (Here it is.) ➡ The end.

There — all done.

Once I've finished my story, my mind → turns to other things, like **DOGZOMBIES** (which is the name of my and Derek's band). I decide to experiment by drawing a few different types of **dogs**

as **ZOMBIES** for a change.

Usually I draw them like this.

Grrrrr

But today I think I'll draw a new one, then a

HUGE
dogzombie,

a bonkers
dogzombie,

a tiny
dogzombie,

a sausage
dogzombie...

I'm just getting started when Mr. Fullerman
STOPS my drawing completely ...

But today I think I'll draw a

Oakfield School
PLANNER

Class........................
Name........................

a tiny
dogzombie,

a sausage
dogzom

I'm just getting started
STOPS my drawing complete

"TOM — as you've **OBVIOUSLY**
finished your story and have
found time for drawing, you
can hand out the **NEW**
school planners to the
class."

"YES, sir."

Sigh.

Marcus Meldrew (who sits next to me) is very IMPATIENT. He sees the new planners and tries to SNATCH one from the pile.

"Give me MY planner, Tom ... hand it over."

Which is a bit rude.

So I say, "Calm down, Marcus, you'll get yours eventually."

Then I take a planner from the top of the pile and pass it over his head right around to AMY PORTER.

Whoops.

"Here we go, AMY—your planner."

This winds Marcus up. He tells me, "Hurry up, I WANT my planner NOW!"

He's tugging at my sweater, which is annoying. So I ignore him and begin giving out the planners from the BACK of the class, working my way to the front.

By the time I reach Marcus, he's practically tearing his hair out with frustration.

"Last but not least—your planner."

Marcus goes to GRAB it from me and Mr. Fullerman says,

"Don't snatch, Marcus."

I agree—so I hand Marcus his planner in
EXTRA s l o w m o t i o n.

(Which is funny and makes Marcus more

CROSS —a double whammy.)

Mr. Fullerman says that if we've finished our stories (like me ☺) we should write our names on the planners, then take a GOOD lᴏᴏk through them and REMIND ourselves of any SPECIAL SCHOOL EVENTS that are coming up this term.

"These planners are for you to write down information. Like when your homework is due."

(Which is not *my* idea of important information.)

I'm flicking through the first few pages of the planner. There's the usual school stuff inside like:

Oakfield School Behavior Policy

(I didn't even know we had one.)

A calendar

School holiday dates 😊

(VERY important.)

Dates for school reports (☹ Not so important.)

School fairs

Sports days

School photographs — blah, blah, blah.

There are also a few blank pages for **NOTES**.

I cross out N̶O̶T̶E̶S̶ and write

 instead. Then I spot

something that I'd completely forgotten about

marked VERY clearly:

Special Events
YEAR FIVE—School Activity Trip

MONDAY

TUESDAY

| WEDNESDAY |

WHICH IS NEWS!

I nudge **AMY** and say, "HEY, I'd forgotten about the **SCHOOL ACTIVITY TRIP!** That's good, isn't it?" and she says,

 "Haven't you put your name down already?"

And I say "NO."

 "Didn't you get the letter WEEKS ago about the trip?"

"Er, NO?"

 "So I'm guessing your parents didn't fill in the form or go to the meeting about the trip either?"

"No and no," I say.

THIS is not sounding promising at all.

Then <u>just</u> when I think things can't get any worse, Marcus joins in the conversation.

"You won't be going then, Tom. It's fully booked up now. Bad luck."

HOW DID THIS HAPPEN?

I'm trying to remember what I did with the VERY important SCHOOL ACTIVITY TRIP LETTER?

Think, think ...

OK, just remembered.

AMY must think I'm some kind of idiot for losing my letter (well, sort of losing it) — groan.

I tell her, "I'm not normally so forgetful."

"Yes you are, Tom," **AMY** says.

(Which is a bit TRUE.)

If I don't get to go on the trip, I'll be missing GOOD stuff like:

☺ climbing (I'm not bad at that)

☺ Swimming (good)

☺ Kayaking (which is a kind of canoeing I've never done before — sounds good)

☺ Building stuff (can't wait)

Every year the kids who've been on the trip ALWAYS come back and tell EVERYONE how FANTASTIC it was.

(Which can be a bit annoying.)

The trip was AMAZING! BRILLIANT! So good!

I really want to go. Sigh.

AMY suggests I talk to Mr. Fullerman about getting another form. Good thinking. ☺
I put my hand up and say,

> Mr. Fullerman, I've just seen the **SCHOOL ACTIVITY TRIP** in my planner – is it too late to put my name down?

Mr. Fullerman looks at me from his desk and says,
"I hope not, Tom. I'll give you another letter. Try not to lose this one, will you?"

(How did he know I'd lost it?)

Break time

When I see my best mate, Derek, at break time, I ask him about the **SCHOOL ACTIVITY TRIP.** He says, "I thought you were going?" I say, "No, I forgot, and now it might be too late."

Derek says, "It won't be as much FUN * without you, Tom."

Which is nice of him, but doesn't help my situation. EVERYONE seems to be going—apart from me.

Solid → ☺ Norman → 😠
Mark ⇨ 😀 Amy → 👧
Indrani → 👩 Florence ⇨ 😊
Brad → 😊 Oh, yes, and Marcus. ⇨ 😠

Every time I 👀 see Marcus, he doesn't stop reminding me that HE'S GOING and I'm **NOT** (YET). 😠

> I'm going on the trip.

And if that's boxed not bad enough, every teacher suddenly seems to want to talk about the **SCHOOL ACTIVITY TRIP** as well.

> *This will be useful if you're going on the* **SCHOOL ACTIVITY TRIP.**

OUTDOOR SPORTS

Mrs. Worthington even says **SCHOOL ACTIVITY TRIP** in MATH!

"The **SCHOOL ACTIVITY TRIP** is for *THREE DAYS*. There are *NINE* different activities to do, so how many could you do each day?"

(The answer is NONE in my case...as I might not be going.)

On the way home, Derek can see I'm a bit fed up. So he tries to make me laugh by telling me what happened in his class today.

"Someone—I don't know **who**—DREW a **FUNNY** picture of Mrs. Nap dressed as a **BEAR** like she did for **Book Week.**"

So I say, "Did you get into trouble, Derek?" (I guessed it was him.)

"It was close, but I managed to RUB out her FACE before Mrs. Nap came in and saw it and told me to SIT down and stop drawing ALIENS on the board!"

Derek shows me a small version of what he drew.

Mrs. Nap

It's genius and does cheer me up. ☺

The **FIRST** and most **IMPORTANT** thing I'm going to do when I get back is to MAKE SURE MOM or DAD fills in my **SCHOOL ACTIVITY TRIP** FORM.

If I forget to bring it in **AGAIN**, I'll have no chance of going.

(Which would be a **DISASTER** for me.)

When I get to my house, I notice there's a group of people standing in next door's front garden. Which is a bit **ODD**.

Mom thinks so too, because I can see 👀 her *peering* through a tiny gap in our living room curtains. She's still "👋" watching them, even when I wave at her.

A very Old lady named Mrs. O'Leary used to live in that house. When I was little, Mrs. O'Leary would tell me that she was ONE HUNDRED AND FIFTY YEARS YOUNG, you know!

I thought it was **TRUE** until Delia pointed out that NOBODY is that old and only an **IDIOT** would believe her.

"That makes you an idiot, Tom," she'd tell me, being a nice sister. 😟

Then a few months ago Mrs. O'Leary moved out BYE! to live closer to her family, leaving the house `empty` until now.

So I'm deliberately taking my time to open MY front door while having a sneaky peek at exactly who's next door.

There's a lady with a clipboard. She's chatting to a man and a lady with a girl (who could be my age, I'm not sure?).

They're all about to go inside when the girl turns around and catches me STARING at her. She SNEERS at me at first ...

THEN she goes and makes

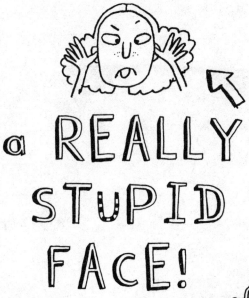

a REALLY STUPID FACE!

huh?

I wasn't expecting that.

Hmmmmmm.

I COULD just ignore her.

OR...

I could do THIS

↓ RIGHT BACK AT HER!

BLAHHHH!!

Then she makes ANOTHER face at
me and sticks out her tongue as well.
I put down my bag and use BOTH hands to
STRETCH down my eyes and pull up ↑
my nose.

(I make a loud UGG! noise
for extra effect.)
UGG!   SO THERE.

Mom's TAPPING on the window, trying to get me to STOP, because EVERYONE'S LOOKING at me now.

Tap tap

Oh

Shame

I want to shout "SHE STARTED IT!" but by the time I've stopped looking at Mom, the lady with the clipboard has already closed the front door and the girl's gone inside.

When I come into the house, Mom looks a bit cross.

"What were you doing making SILLY faces, Tom?"

The girl STARTED it!

Mom says, "That's NO excuse. You should have IGNORED her instead of joining in MAKING SUCH a

HORRIBLE FACE!"

Delia is back from college early and CREEPS in at EXACTLY the same time that Mom says, "HORRIBLE FACE!"

Which is not good timing because straightaway she LAUGHS and says,

"I agree...it's a HORRIBLE FACE."

"Go away, Delia—Mom wasn't talking about that."

"What—your HORRIBLE FACE?"

Mom corrects Delia by saying, "Tom was making a HORRIBLE face, he hasn't got a horrible FACE."

37

"That's a matter of **opinion**," she says.

"Ok, enough!" Mom says. Then she adds, "Anyway, far more importantly, we've got people looking at the house next door."

"New neighbors?" Delia asks.

"I'm not sure yet," says Mom.

Mom is being extra NOSY. She suggests that NOW might be a good time for her to hang out some laundry in the garden.

(Which really means Mom wants to snoop and listen in what they're saying.)

But that's OK because while Mom's trying to spy on the neighbors, I can disappear up to my room with a packet of snacks.
It's messier than usual because I was a bit late going to school this morning. **I**'m digging around trying to find that FORM **M**r. Fullerman gave me. (I'm sure it's in my bag.) I get sidetracked by TWO SWEETS that have slipped down into the lining. I can FEEL them there ... I just need to find out how to GET them ...

left a bit right a bit· NEARLY ... done it.

YUM, unexpected SWEETS are the best! They're almost as good as finding another layer of chocolates that no one's eaten yet.

YES!

The sweet wrappers are a bit **STiCKY** so I'm trying to pick them off carefully when I notice I can see right into next door's garden. It's been empty for a while—I hadn't really looked much before. The man outside is pointing at the ROOF while the other lady is looking around the garden.

That RUDE-face girl is busy hitting flower heads with her stick.

(Mom won't like that.)

She's been outside hanging up <u>ONE</u> tea towel for **AGES** while trying to peer over the fence and listen in at the same time.

I'm still watching when Delia comes out to ask Mom a question. Knowing Delia, it's probably something like,

Can I have some money?

Then Delia glances up at the window and catches me staring at her. She MOUTHS the words

HORRID FACE at

me and shakes her head.

OK, Delia, I'll show YOU what a **REALLY** horrid face looks like. I press mine RIGHT up against the glass until my nose gets completely squashed (that way she'll be able to see all the way up it). My eyes go all WONKY and I get a flat face too. Serves her right. I get a bit carried away **squishing** my face against the window ...

(41)

and forget all about **M**om.

And the new neighbors, who are

l**öö**king at me

AGAIN.

(Groan.)

Mom stops hanging out the

tea towel and comes back into the house.

I have to promise **NOT** to make any more

faces.

Yes, Mom.

We're both upstairs when the doorbell

rings (which gets me off the hook).

It's Granddad **B**ob, who's just

popped on his mobility scooter for a visit

while Granny Mavis

is shopping.

Hello.

Tra-
-la-
la!

M om offers him a cup of ☕ tea, and I follow them because in our house:

TEA + Granddad = BISCUITS

🙂 G randdad Bob asks, "Who were all those people coming out of the house next door?"

M om says, "P ossibly our new neighbors — or **not**, if Tom's annoyed them."

🙂 G randdad says, "That young girl was a bit cheeky. She stuck out her tongue and started to make SILLY faces at me for no reason at all."

And straightaway I say,

"See, Mom? That's what she did to me too." ← Girl

Then Mom says, "Yes, but I told you not to make a SILLY face back at her, Tom, didn't I?"

Granddad says, "Hey, Tom, I bet your silly face wasn't as good as the one I made!" Mom is looking at Granddad and shaking her head. Granddad's faces are VERY impressive.

Mom says, "Please tell me YOU didn't make that face in front of our NEW neighbors. Did you?"

That will be a **YES**, then.

My granddad is a **legend**.

Oakfield School
PLANNER
Class............
Name............

My school planner is supposed to REMIND me of IMPORTANT dates and events that are going on in school.

And the *KITCHEN calendar* is where FAMILY stuff like birthdays 🎂 and holidays ☼ are all written down so EVERYONE can see what's happening (and won't forget).

Groan

Most of the time, I find out what's going on like ↓ this ↓.

TOM, GO AND GET

READY FOR _ _ _ _ _ _ _ _ _ _ _.

Fill in the blank here.

It could be a visit to see the cousins , or Auntie Alice's 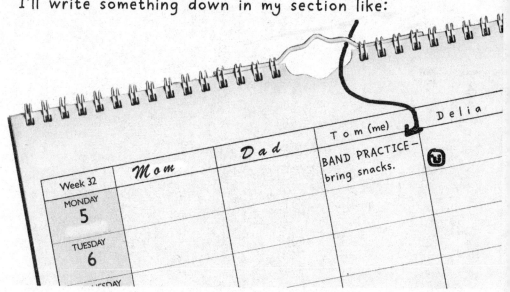 birthday. Occasionally I'll write something down in my section like:

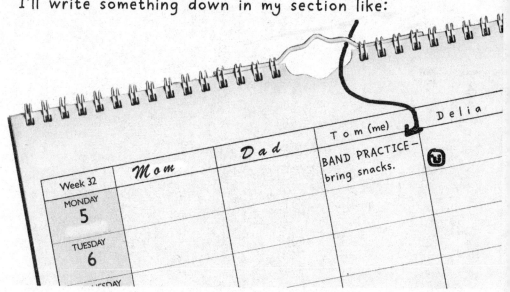

Week 32	Mom	Dad	Tom (me)	Delia
MONDAY 5			BAND PRACTICE— bring snacks.	
TUESDAY 6				

But Mom still ends up having to remind me about it.

BAND PRACTICE— bring snacks.

Sometimes I have FUN writing extra stuff in other people's sections. Like this: ➡

Week 32	M o m	D a d	T o m (me)	D e l i a
			BAND PRACTICE – bring snacks.	
MONDAY **5**	Shopping			
TUESDAY **6**	pick up Granny Mavis from YOGA			
WEDNESDAY **7**		Work in evening		
THURSDAY **8**				
FRIDAY **9**				
SATURDAY **10**		FITNESS PROGRAM starts today		
SUNDAY **11**		And ends HERE Ha! Ha!		

It's taken Dad a WHOLE week
to spot this one.

huh?

He tells me,

"I'll have you know, Tom, that RIGHT NOW my body is a TEMPLE."

Then he starts doing lots of really embarrassing muscle-man poses.

Mom's laughing at Dad posing. She says, "More like a Temple of Doom," then brings out the shopping list and crosses off BISCUITS for Frank.

BISCUITS
(for Frank)
Milk
Butter
Eggs

"I'm assuming you don't want me to buy biscuits that might ruin your 'TEMPLE,' Frank?"

Dad tells us, It takes a lot of hard work to look this good, you know.

Mom and I leave him flexing his muscles and pretending to do push-ups on the wall while we head off to the **SUPERMARKET.**

100-101-102

Oh, dear

Normally I would [avoid] shopping with Mom —
but for some reason,
FOOD shopping isn't quite
so bad.

MMMM, CAKES.

In the CAR, Mom's about to drive off
when Uncle Kevin pulls up next to us.

He hops out to say hello, so Mom opens her
window.

Hi, Rita!

He says, "I was just passing, so I thought I'd
check that everything's still OK?"

Mom looks puzzled. "Everything's GREAT, thanks, Kevin."

"It's very good of you to help out, Rita." From the LOOK on Mom's face, I can tell she has NO idea what Uncle Kevin's talking about. But she still says,

"Of course, it's NO problem, Kevin." Then Uncle Kevin asks ME, "Are you sure you don't mind, Tom?"

Mom's giving me the EVILS in case I say something stupid—like, "We've got NO idea what you're talking about, Uncle Kevin."

(Which wouldn't be the first time.)

So I just play along and say,

"I don't mind at all."

Luckily Uncle Kevin adds, "The boys are really looking forward to staying over with you."

And SUDDENLY Mom remembers what's happening. "Of course! It's ALL on the *kitchen calendar*."

(It's not.)

Uncle Kevin looks at his watch.

"I'll go and say hello to Frank while I'm here."

"We've just left him FLEXING all his muscles," Mom tells him.

"That shouldn't take too long, then!"

Uncle Kevin is still LAUGHING at his joke when we drive off. Mom says to me, "Your dad will be surprised to see Uncle Kevin, won't he?"

(Yes he will.)

SUPERMARKET Special

Part of going food shopping with **M**om is being able to *sneak* a few "extra snacks" into the cart when she's not looking. → → →↘↘↓

I don't always get to keep them, though.

I'm only buying essentials, Tom.

Custard creams ARE essential.

I spend most of the car journey telling **M**om how WELL I did in school this week (for a change). Fingers crossed she'll be in a REALLY good mood and happy to treat me.

I don't tell her the **WHOLE** story about how

MARCUS MELDREW tried to distract

 my reading by `STARING` at me with his

EYES → CROSSED. (Mom doesn't need to

hear about any more

funny faces.)

BESIDES, I played a good ⚡trick⚡ on

Marcus later that day and pretended his

EYES ◌̀ ◌ were ⊂⊃ ⊂⊃ crossed **AGAIN**.

"Uncross your eyes, Marcus," I told him.

"They're not crossed," he said.

"They REALLY are ... and if you don't

UNCROSS them, they might stay like that

FOREVER."

"**H**ow come I can only SEE **O**NE of you if they're CROSSED, then?" he asked me.

So I told him, "**THAT'S** a VERY **BAD** sign. It means your eyes are starting to **STICK** like that already."

(I was very convincing.)

Marcus wanted to see for himself, so he asked to go to the restroom. **W**hen he came back, he said, "My eyes are FINE. I'm not falling for THAT trick again."

I pointed out that he must have **WOBBLED** them back into place when he stood up. Ha! Ha!

(Mom didn't need to hear any of that stuff.)

57

So here I am at the **SUPERMARKET** with
Mom and her LIST (which she likes to try
to STICK to).

M om says, "Thank goodness
Uncle Kevin reminded me about
your cousins coming to stay.

I have NO idea WHEN they're coming,
though. Not too soon, I hope."
(Me too.)
"I'll look on the *kitchen calendar* – it MUST
be written down." It's definitely NOT,
and I know why.

Huh?

Hello, Kevin.
Of course they can come
and STAY. I'm writing it
on the calendar now.

We grab a cart and head to the **FRUIT** and **VEGETABLE** section.

There's a *Special Offer*

on a **BIG SUPER SAVER** BAG OF **BANANAS**.

 Mom puts one in the cart and says,

"Bit green, but they'll ripen up."

Normally I would wait for a good covering of shopping on the bottom of the cart before attempting to sneak in a treat.

But I don't have the chance because Mom has brought out ANOTHER ...

"I nearly forgot, I've got this mini list for you to do if that's OK, Tom?"

OWN LIST + OWN CART = OWN TREATS

Yes, Mom, I can do that.

"I'll be here so come straight back, no messing around, OK?"

It's not a **BIG SUPERMARKET** – I know where to go, so this won't take long.

I like being in charge of my own cart.

60

On the **list** I have to get:

o Cereal —that's easy ✓

o Chocolate spread *Spread* ✓

(NOT on the list but a BARGAIN)

o Fizzy sherbet ✓

(not on the list, but

for the cousins)

o Onion rings ✓

(not on the list—for

me and the cousins)

o BAG of SELF-RISING FLOUR—whatever ✓

o BAG of SUGAR—check ✓

(Shopping is a *breeze*.)

o SUPERSIZE PACKAGE OF TOILET PAPER

(largest pack)

I'm looking up and down the aisle
and I had NO IDEA there were SO many . . .

different types!

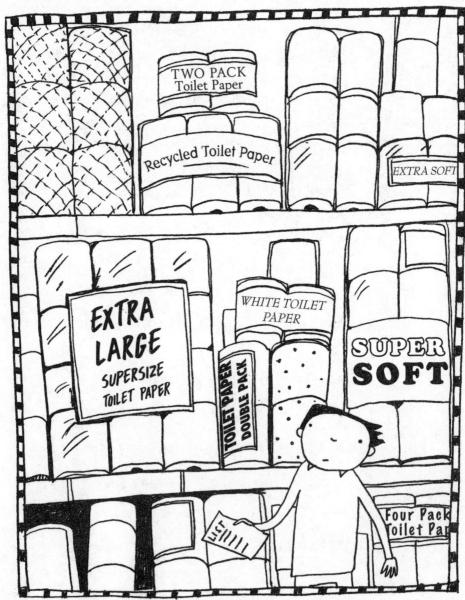

Quilted, extra soft, recycled, extra thick, budget, packs of two-six-twelve, different colors.

I read the list again—SUPERSIZE, it says. But they all look the same size to me?

I'm confused.

Until I spot the **BIGGEST** pack I've ever seen.

(Yep, that's them.) ⟹

I try to lift a pack down from the shelf. It's not heavy, just tricky to hold. I'm struggling to carry it and I can't quite see ⊙ ⊙ where I'm going or where I left my cart?

It's here somewhere—here we go.

SUPER SIZE

EXTRA LARGE SUPER TOILET

EXTRA LARGE SUPERSIZE TOILET PAPER

I SQUASH the MASSIVE pack of toilet paper down into the cart and head back to where Mom is.

On the way I make a quick detour to grab a pack of caramel wafers and wedge them down the back. THERE—all done. ☺

I can hear someone calling

Tom! It must be Mom, so I do a super-spin turn in the cart and BUMP right into...

"What are you doing here, Amy?" I say.

AMY says, "Same as you, Tom...or I WAS until you stole my cart."

"HUH! DID I?"

"YES, you did. I saw you. Our groceries are under that MASSIVE pack of toilet paper."

"Oh, yes...so they are."

EXTRA LARGE SUPERSIZE TOILET PAPER

(That's embarrassing.)

"**We** need to swap carts, then—
follow me."

(I feel like I'm doing the **SUPERMARKET** walk
of SHAME.)

AMY says, "That's a LOT of toilet paper."
(**Oh, great**—as if this wasn't AWKWARD
enough, I have to chat about TOILET PAPER too.)
So I just say, "It was on my list."
And wave my list at her.

LIST

AMY's mom is chatting with my mom,
who's standing next to my cart, which is
FULL of stuff that's NOT on the list.

AMY's mom says,
"It's easily done, don't worry, Tom!"

"I wondered why you were taking a while,"
Mom says. (She's spotted all the extra goodies
I have.)

I say, "It's all for the cousins....
OK, some stuff's for me."

AMY says, "You've squished our
tomatoes and bread, Tom."

(Whoops—so I have.)

AMY's mom says, "We'll get more."

Luckily the toilet paper hasn't squished my caramel wafers.

I grab the wafers and shove them into our cart behind the toilet paper again. Only somehow I manage to accidentally *rip* the plastic that's holding the rolls together. Two of them fall out

and BOUNCE on the ---ground.

Then they KEEP ROLLING right down past all the checkouts, building up speed as they go.

"QUICKLY, TOM, GRAB THEM!" Mom shouts.

I'm trying! I manage to catch them before they unravel completely.

(All this in front of Amy too.)

I just want to go home now.

But we STILL have to pay at the checkout.

The man on the register asks Mom,

"This toilet-paper pack is broken;

do you want a new one?"

And Mom says,

"Thank you, that would be good."

The man announces to the WHOLE

SUPERMARKET through a loudspeaker:

"SUPERSIZE PACK OF
TOILET PAPER to register SIX, PLEASE.
THE REALLY ENORMOUS
PACK. THE PACK THAT LOOKS
LIKE IT WILL LAST FOR ...
ABOUT A YEAR?"

That's not true—but he thinks it's funny.

(I've had enough of toilet paper for one day.)

We're loading up the car with the groceries when we bump into **AMY** and her mom **AGAIN.** Mom is busy trying to **FIT** all the toilet paper into the trunk (which won't close). So she starts passing me individual rolls to put on the back seat. (It's like playing a game of toilet-paper hot potato.)

AMY says, "Those rolls are a lot of trouble, aren't they?"

I say, "YES—they are."

Then I suddenly remember something that's NOT a lot of trouble. My ⟩caramel wafers⟨ I take them out of the bag and offer **AMY** one. "**G**ood thing I remembered to take these out of your cart!" I tell her. **AMY** says, "Thanks, Tom. Did you remember to turn in your **SCHOOL ACTIVITY TRIP** form as well?"

"NO!"

It's been nearly a WHOLE week since Mr. Fullerman gave me another form to fill in (which must still be in my room somewhere).

As we drive home, Mom tells me not to worry. She says, "There's nothing you can do about it now, Tom. I'll fill it in when we get back."

That's the plan.

Back at home, I go and search for my

Form straightaway. I think it's buried in

my MESSY room.... Well, I hope it is?

At last! It's under a pile of

ROCK WEEKLYS. I take it downstairs

and Mom fills it all in while Dad

No biscuits?

unpacks all the groceries.

Mom makes a suggestion.

"So you don't miss the trip,

why don't I pop into school with the form and

have a quick WORD with someone?"

"What sort of word do you want to have?" I

ask Mom (thinking the worst).

"Don't worry, Tom, I'll ask Mr. Fullerman or

Mrs. Mumble about the trip very nicely. We

don't want you to miss out."

Then (as usual) Delia manages to turn up and

join in the conversation.

She adds, "And MUCH more importantly, we want to get rid of you for a few days."

"That's not true," Mom says.

"OK . . . for a few weeks, then."

(I ignore her.)

Dad wants to know why we've bought SO many bananas?

Mom says, "We're going to have lots of visitors. So don't worry, they'll all get eaten."

Then Delia says unless we've got a family of chimps coming for tea we might struggle to eat THAT many bananas — which annoys Mom a bit.

"They were on SALE –
I'm trying not to spend too much."

Delia says, "Speaking of money,
can I borrow some for bus fare?"

Mom and Dad forget about the
bananas and tell Delia that:

1. She can't keep asking them for
money all the time.

Can I have
some money?

2. She's old enough to get a Saturday job.

I'm standing behind Mom and
Dad nodding in agreement, which
would normally drive Delia . . .

BANANAS. Ha!
Ha!

But today she just says,

"Please can I have some money — or I'll be **LATE**."

And Mom says, **"LATE** for WHAT? You didn't tell us you were going out. **I**t's not written on the *calendar*."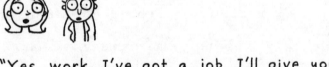

Now I'm wagging my finger at her.

Delia says, "I'll be late for **work**."

WORK? Mom and Dad look shocked.

"Yes, work. I've got a job. I'll give you the money back when I get paid," she tells them.

Mom wants to know where she's working (and so do I).

"At a food place in town—only for a few hours. But it's a job, so be happy, OK?"

Dad hands over some money with his mouth open. Delia *rushes off* and leaves them both looking a bit surprised.

I take the opportunity to sneak in (what I think is) a very good suggestion.

"Now that you don't have to worry about Delia, does that mean there's more pocket money for me?"

I'll take that as a NO, then.
(Worth a try, though.)

Mom says I have to clean my room JUST IN CASE the cousins turn up to stay. Hello.

I agree to clean a bit.

As I'm SQUEEZING a few things under my bed (which does the trick for now),

I see Derek in his room from my window.

He holds up a card with a very good idea on it.

Game of MONSTER BATTLESHIP?

I hold up a sign that says ...

It's a useful game in situations when you're a bit bored but need to keep QUIET.

Once in a particularly LONG and boring assembly, we played it sitting at the back of the hall.

It's like **normal** Battleship only with **MONSTERS** instead.

Here's how we play it:

There's a KING monster – worth 20 points.

And a QUEEN monster – worth another 20 points.

Then there are five mini monsters – worth 5 points each.

And five BLOB monsters – each worth 1 point.

You draw a square and number them like this:

Then you draw all your monsters in different squares.

= B9 · E7 · G2 · G8 · G9   = D5

= D3 · E2 · E3 · E8 · G3   = I7

$\mathcal{D}$erek writes down what square he's going for and holds it up to the window.

He's already HIT one of my monsters! AGGGH!

Then it's my turn.

(I missed.)

He's got another one of my monsters!

$\mathcal{W}$e keep playing until Derek's mom comes in and says he has to go to bed. Derek won this time.

MORNING! Down at breakfast, Mom and Dad are asking me if I have any idea where Delia is working?

I say, "No, but I'm sure I can find out!"

Straightaway Mom says, "I don't want you snooping around in your sister's room, Tom."

Dad LAUGHS and says, "Absolutely [not], Tom—that's your MOTHER'S job."

Then Mom says, "What do you mean? I'm not a nosy person at all!"
(But I can think of loads of times she's been a bit nosy!)

So I say, "What about when you were pretending to hang out laundry so you could hear what the NEW next-door neighbors were talking about?"

Mom says, "I had lots of wet laundry to hang out. I wasn't pretending!"

So I remind her that she only had ONE tea towel. Which makes Dad LAUGH.

"When did we get new neighbors?" he asks. I tell him how they were looking around the house next door and how the little girl was REALLY annoying. "For no reason at all, she KEPT on making faces at me ...like this ..." (I demonstrate.)

Delia comes down for breakfast and says, "That's a **BIG** improvement, Tom, you should stay like that."

(Very funny, Delia.)

Dad says,

"Morning, Miss I've Got a Job."

Which makes Delia say, (Oh, pleeease.)

Mom asks her where she's working again.

Delia says, "What does it matter? If I tell you, I know what will happen. The **WHOLE** family will turn up to **BUG** me."

(THAT'S a good idea. I REALLY want to find out now.)

Delia says grumpily, "I'm going now — and I'll be late getting home tonight because I'm **WORKING**."

Mom starts shoving bananas at her as she
leaves.

Groan

"Take one for a snack.
Take two."

I've just noticed my cereal is covered
with chopped bananas as well. Which is not
how I'd normally have cereal, but I don't mind.
I like bananas.

Just as well, really. We've got LOADS.

My **SCHOOL ACTIVITY TRIP** form is on the fridge with a LARGE STICKY note that says DON'T FORGET (so I won't forget).

I manage to persuade Mom NOT to come into school for a word after all. There's no way I'll forget my form now, because Mom's stuck reminder notes

EVERYWHERE I look.

Derek POPS by to see if I'm ready to go to school yet. You ready yet? (Not quite; nearly.)

While I'm upstairs brushing my teeth, Dad's chatting to Derek downstairs.

"Are you going on the school trip, Derek?"

"I hope so."

Then I hear Mom asking Derek if he can:

1. Make sure I turn in my form?

2. Take a banana with him?

"We've got plenty."

It's like Mom doesn't trust me! Which is annoying.

I RUN downstairs and grab my bag for school. Then Derek and I both say

BYE! before rushing out the door. We're only halfway down the road when the look on my face tells Derek that ... NOOOOOOOO!

Mom's waiting for me at the door
with the form in her hand.
(Along with another banana
in case I get hungry.) Got it!

At school, Mr. Fullerman says I can
take my form to the office.
So straightaway I go off to see
Mrs. Mumble, who's on the phone.
While I'm waiting for her to finish her call,
a family comes in and stands behind me. Mrs.
Mumble puts her hand over the phone and says,

"I'm sorry, I'll be
with you in a minute.
Please take a seat."

Not to me – to the family
behind me, who all go and sit
down. I turn around to have a look.

There's a GIRL who looks very familiar?

As I'm staring at her ... she starts doing stupid bunny teeth at me.

NOW I REMEMBER! ➡️

What's SHE doing here in my school?

Mrs. Mumble gets off the phone.

"What's this, Tom?" I give her the form but I get a bit distracted by the GIRL and BLURT OUT ...

It's my ACTIVITY RABBIT FORM, Mrs. Mumble.

Which makes no sense at all.

"Do you mean your

SCHOOL ACTIVITY TRIP form, Tom?"

"YES."

"It's a bit late. But we've had a few cancellations so you might be OK."

I tell Mrs. Mumble that I'm sorry it's late but I really want to go and if she can do anything to make sure that I'm on the list that would be ABSOLUTELY AMAZING.

She says, "Like I said, Tom, you might be in luck with the cancellations."

Which is EXCELLENT NEWS.

Then Mrs. Mumble says to the waiting family, "Welcome to Oakfield School! Mr. Keen will be with you very soon."

I hope that girl's not coming to MY school! And if she is, fingers crossed she's not in my class.

That would be BAD NEWS—unless she sat next to Marcus and annoyed him instead. (Which might work?)

With my form SAFELY handed in, I go back to class to catch up on one of my favorite subjects.

ART

(Things are looking up!)

Mrs. Worthington is teaching our lesson today. "Put down paper all over the desks so they don't get too messy."

Mrs. Worthington wants us to get a brush, a water pot, and one color of paint to do our pictures. (Less paint to clean up, I suppose?)

Norman Watson is already in trouble for FLICKiNG paint onto his paper.

Most of it's gone on Pansy's back.

Stop flicking paint, Norman!

Next Mrs. Worthington says, "Find a lovely object to paint using the techniques I've just shown you. If you want to take anything from the table over there to paint, please do."
(Mmmmm, not really.)
"Or you might have something of your own instead?"

That's an idea. Shame I didn't bring any caramel wafers with me today.

I'm rummaging through my bag and I find a couple of toothpicks left over from the cheese and banana hedgehog Granny brought over.

And I find ANOTHER banana.

Granny's
banana hedgehog

I Poke the picks into the banana so it looks a bit like an alien. AMY brings a small plant back to the table and for SOME reason Marcus has chosen a woolly SOCK with individual toes to paint.

Mrs. Worthington is walking around, giving tips on what to do next. "*Good start on your sock, Marcus.*"
Marcus suddenly moves his arm and BUMPS me.

I SPLODGE paint all over my paper just when Mrs. Worthington comes to look at it.

"*Mmmm, interesting combination, Tom.*"

I try to tell her what happened. "It was a mistake.... Marcus bumped ..."

But Mrs. Worthington's already gone to stop Norman from **FLiCKing** more paint.

I say, "Thanks a lot, Marcus, for bumping me." He says, "I didn't touch you! It's not my fault your picture looks like a

SPLODGE."

Mmmmm, this splodge reminds me of someone.

"Can you guess who this is, Amy?" I ask her.

She guesses straightaway.

Ha! Ha! Ha! Ha!

While I'm waiting for my picture to DRY,

I take the ⎯⎯⎯ toothpicks out of the banana and { think } about eating it.

That's when I notice that the banana skin has turned **BLACK** where the tooth-picks went in.

I gently poke one of the picks into the skin again—and it starts to turn **black** almost right away. OK—this could be good.

So I do a few more dots and start to build up a doodle.

Watch out for pointy ends of pick!

AMY wonders what I'm doing, so I show her.

"That's AMAZING," she says.

It's good, isn't it?

I do another banana doodle on the fresh side.

Guess who!

AMY is very impressed and thinks it's **FUNNY**. And Marcus, who's being nosy, is looking at it too.

"What's that?"

"A banana **doodle.**"
"Let's have a look," he says.

Marcus wants to know how I did it.
So I say, "It's easy, I'll show you."

Dot dot dot dot dot dot dot dot ... dot.

"There you go. That's how you do it."

Marcus is studying the banana closely. As the dots get darker, he says, "OK, I get it now....

Is THAT MRS. WORTHINGTON?

So I say, "Keep your voice down, Marcus. I don't want Mrs. Worthington to see it."

See what, Tom?

(Too late.)

Mrs. Worthington says, "That's very creative, Tom. You've done a DOT drawing on a banana..." (I have.) "And that looks a bit like me?"

Uh-oh, I'm in trouble now....

103

"Stay behind after class, Tom."

(I'm guessing Mrs. Worthington has just seen the extra mustache dots.)

Groan.

(Could have been worse, I suppose.)

EVEN MORE bananas News... has traveled

FAST about my banana tattoos and how to do them.

Bananas have never been so popular in school.

They're everywhere!

I've been doing a few **extra** banana

doodles at home too. (You can still eat the

banana as long as you don't leave them for

TOO long.)

This one is for **D**elia.

I told her it was a

present. Ha! Ha!

The pile of bananas Mom bought was gradually going down when Granny Mavis came over with a WHOLE lot more.

"Hello! I know how much you all like bananas and they were SUCH a good value."

(Luckily she didn't bring another one of her banana hedgehogs.)

But she had made some banana and pepper biscuits.

Norman and Derek turned up for band practice just in time to eat some.

We're supposed to be writing new songs for **DOGZOMBIES**. But it's so easy to get distracted. Granny gives us a plate of biscuits to take up to my room with us. Norman eats most of them.

I get out my guitar and TRY to think of things we could write songs about. Norman suggests How about bananas?

Maybe (maybe not).

"Or about a dog called Rooster?" Derek says because we can all hear him BARKING in the garden.

Norman wonders if our favorite band in the **WHOLE** world — **DUDE 3** — would write about a pet dog?

So far the songwriting is **NOT** going very well.

We have a few more ideas from

looking at stuff around my room.

Pillow song

Blanket song

I see through the WINDOW.

Window song

Then I suggest we could look at the pile of

ROCK WEEKLYS for inspiration?

"Delia's got more in her room, I'll get them,"
I tell them. They agree.

It's a **GREAT IDEA.**

I think Delia's at work (wherever work is), so she won't catch me snooping around.

While I'm in there, I spot something that looks **VERY** **ODD** and out of place in Delia's room.

It's a little white **HAT**. I've **NEVER** seen her wear anything like that before.

I grab the **ROCK WEEKLYS** and put the hat on my head.

Norman and **D**erek think it looks stupid on me.

It looks stupid on them too.

As we're looking through the **ROCK WEEKLYS**, this **PAGE** GETS MY ATTENTION.

CALLING ALL DUDE3 FANS!

Here's your chance to design a T-shirt for **DUDE3**.

DUDE3 is looking to their fans to come up with an original design for a T-SHIRT that will be printed and WORN by the band themselves.

Send your designs to the address below

with your name,

address,

and contact details.

Competition deadline is

Songwriting is abandoned (for now). Instead I get out all my pens, paint, and paper and we all have a go at doing some T-shirt designs. Norman's paint FLICking works out a bit better this time.

Derek's drawing is pretty good too.

My doodle T-shirt design takes a while—worth it, though.

Dad pops his head around the door to see how the songwriting is going.

(It's not.)

T hen he says,

> I've got a special tasty snack for you all too. Three guesses what it is?

 Not more bananas, I say. Groan.

Bananas . . . with a difference.

Dad's gone and stuck a wafer on each of them. Thanks, Dad!

(It's a very good idea.)

H e likes our T-shirts too.

N orman tries to eat his while Derek and I go straight for the wafers. We save the bananas for later (after I've done another quick doodle on them). We're just finishing off our T-shirt designs when Delia comes STORMING into my room. She SHOUTS,

 Where's my HAT?

So I say, "What hat?"

"The **ONE** you took from my room, along with those **ROCK WEEKLYS** too," she says, looking at all her magazines.

I try to keep a straight face and tell her,

"No hats around here."

(Derek and Norman are keeping OUT of this.)

"I need it for WORK—so you better give it back FAST."

Then Delia suddenly spots her hat...

the bananas are wearing it.

Delia snatches the hat back and shouts, "Keep OUT of my room!"

I wait until Delia's left before making Derek
and Norman L A U G H like this.

Ha! Ha!

SCHOOL NEWS!

In class, Mr. Fullerman says he has an announcement to make.

Lŏ ō king at the expression on his face, I can't tell if it's going to be

GOOD news, BAD news, or both?

So we're all waiting ... and waiting ... "It's about the school trip," he says.

(He's really stringing this out ...)

"If you've put your name down on the list, I can tell you now that you ..."

(YES, what!)

"You'll ..."

WHAT!

"ALL be going on the trip."

PHEW! That is GOOD news.

It's not long before we go either, so that's just as well. Then he tells us (and here comes the BAD news bit), **"Everyone will be expected to take notes on all the interesting experiences you'll be having on the trip."**

Really?

"Each of you will be given a VERY special journal to write in."

(And hopefully draw in too?)

Mr. Fullerman shows us some of the journals that other kids have done in the past.

(They're a bit good.)

"As you can see, it's a GREAT way of remembering your trip."

Mmmm, I guess so. Sounds like a lot of work to me. The journals are a bit nicer than our usual schoolbooks — which is good. . . . And there's no other homework to do while we're writing our journals. EXCELLENT!

Mr. Fullerman hands out more LETTERS about the trip too.

There's a LIST of STUFF we have to bring. The only thing I don't have is a waterproof coat, but Derek has two so I can borrow one of his.

At break time I double-check that's OK with Derek. (No problem.) PHEW!

I say, "That means I won't have to go clothes shopping with Mom." ⬇ Which is always a relief.

Derek asks me if Delia is still MAD at me. And I say, "She is, but that HAT has made me want to know where she works even MORE."

This is cute, Tom.

Not for me.

(I'll have to find out when I get back from my trip—Mom and Dad really want to know too.)

I've also noticed now that I'm definitely going on the TRIP —not one teacher has mentioned it in any of my lessons! (When before, they wouldn't stop going on about it!)

Which is annoying, because I'm so excited I can't stop thinking about the trip...

in class...

and at home.

But Mom and Dad are driving me a bit BONKERS about the trip.

You'll need lots of extra-warm VESTS.

Sigh.

You can take this woolly hat with you, Tom.

Oh, great.

I'm only going for **THREE DAYS,**

but from the way Mom's fussing about things

I have to pack, you'd think it was

THREE WEEKS!

Box of bandages

All your PANTS

And toothpaste

Extra socks

Delia's been out a **LOT** and I haven't seen

that HAT→ again since the bananas were

wearing it.

As I'm off tomorrow on the trip,

THE FOSSILS have come over to say BYE.

Granny Mavis says,

"I've made you a little

something."

(Which is nice of her.)

It doesn't look like a little I present to me?

It's not. ➡️

Granny's knitted me a HUGE sweater with a MASSIVE smiling banana on the front!

"You'll grow into it, Tom. It'll keep you warm on your trip," she tells me.

"Thanks, Granny," I say. I don't mention it might not fit in my bag. Granddad gives me some banana biscuits "for travel snacks."

He bites into one and pretends it's broken his teeth.

Which makes Granny sigh.

crack

I give them both a HUG and go off to pack the rest of my stuff.

121

I discover that (SOMEHOW) Mom has managed to sneakily pack my bag already.

SURPRISE
ALL done! Mom x

So I just need to concentrate on the **really important** stuff instead (my snacks).

Some of the other things Mom wanted me to take — I leave out.

Tom Snacks

Shower cap?

Eye mask?

(I keep the bandages. They might be handy.)

Tonight I'm going to bed EARLY. I don't want to be late (as usual).

I'm **very EXCITED.**

Mustn't forget to bring my ACTIVITY trip journal either.

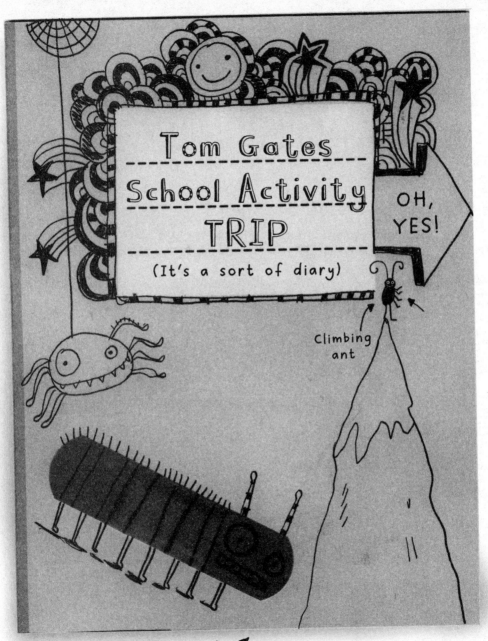

Tom Gates
School Activity
TRIP
(It's a sort of diary)

OH, YES!

Climbing ant

Bandages are useful already.

AWAKE!

The Journey

Just for a CHANGE I managed to wake up NICE and EARLY so I could:

1. Get into the bathroom B.D.
   (which stands for BEFORE DELIA)

2. Double-check I hadn't forgotten anything important for my trip (like my swimming trunks — because THAT'S happened before)

3. Make a VERY BIG decision — teddy or no teddy?
   (I decided to bring teddy — but hide him.)
   Then I SQUEEZED my bag shut and headed downstairs for breakfast. ☺

I was in a really GOOD mood until I bumped ¿ into Delia coming out of her room. She *pushed* past me and said,

Haven't you gone yet?

Which I thought was a stupid question to ask. So I told her, "If I'd GONE, I wouldn't be here, would I?"

Then she said, "Well hurry up and go, will you?"—before accidentally *TRIPPING* over some cans of paint and brushes that Dad had left at the bottom of the stairs.

Dad was in the kitchen and called OUT:

MIND the cans of paint and the brushes at the bottom of the stairs

just a little bit **too** late.

Enjoy your *trip?* I asked Delia. Which I thought was FUNNY even if she didn't. Ha!

I left my bag at the front door, then headed to the kitchen, where I could

Smell something DELICIOUS being cooked.

It was **PANCAKES!** MY FAVORITE. ☺

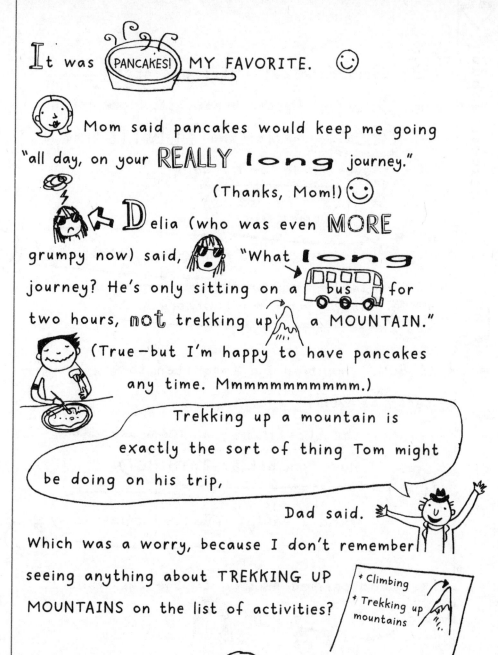

Mom said pancakes would keep me going "all day, on your REALLY **long** journey."

(Thanks, Mom!) ☺

Delia (who was even MORE grumpy now) said, "What **long** journey? He's only sitting on a bus for two hours, **not** trekking up a MOUNTAIN."

(True—but I'm happy to have pancakes any time. Mmmmmmmmmmm.)

Trekking up a mountain is exactly the sort of thing Tom might be doing on his trip,

Dad said.

Which was a worry, because I don't remember seeing anything about TREKKING UP MOUNTAINS on the list of activities?

* Climbing
* Trekking up mountains

(I decided to eat THREE pancakes just in case.) After breakfast, Mom asked me for the **TENTH** time if I'd got everything, and I said,

YES, I've got EVERYTHING.

Even your toothbrush?

 Apart from my toothbrush.

(I didn't mention I'd forgotten to brush my teeth as well.)

For the ELEVENTH time Mom asked me,

Have you got EVERYTHING?

And I said, YES...I think so.

Then Dad carried my bag to the car while I said BYE to Delia.

"**A**re you **STILL** here?" she asked.

 "**I**'m leaving now." **Finally,**

Delia said grumpily.

Then she stood by the front door to watch us go.

When I got in the car, Mom told me, "We'll miss you, Tom. Even Delia will miss you!"

But from the way Delia was PUNCHING the air and pretending to celebrate as we drove off, I'm **not** so sure. ➡ —Yes

When we got to school, everyone was already sitting on the bus waiting for me.

Hurry up, Tom, you're a bit late,

Mr. Fullerman told me as we arrived.

Being late wasn't such a BAD thing because Mom and Dad had to say goodbye to me quickly without too much fussing or hugging. (Phew.)

BYE!

All the kids in my class were watching,

including Marcus Meldrew. Who for some reason was STARING at me with his EYES CROSSED (again).

Derek managed to save me a seat behind Solid and Norman, who was so excited he could hardly keep still.

When the bus finally set off, all our moms, dads, friends, families, and even pets waved goodbye.

All the kids CHEERED and waved back. (Apart from Julia Morton, who was already feeling carsick.)

The SCHOOL ACTIVITY TRIP had begun!

HOORAY!

Straightaway, Derek and I got out our snacks to see what we both had to eat. It was an **excellent** selection.

Derek said, "This FEAST will last us for **AGES**."

Before

After

(It didn't.)

Most of the girls, were sitting including **AMY PORTER**, were sitting together at the back of the bus and

SINGING REALLY LOUDLY.

Normally, Mr. Fullerman would get cr**o**ss and say, **That's enough singing, girls.** OR **Too loud!**

But as this was supposed to be a **"FUN TRIP"** he let them keep singing ♫ (for a while, anyway).

Derek suggested we could play that **YES or NO** game. Which was a good idea, as Derek had come prepared with sticky notes and everything.

He wrote something down quickly and stuck it to my forehead.

(133)

Solid was already LAUGHING at what it said. "That's a good one," he told me. Which made it MUCH harder for me to think of something good that Derek could be. I thought I'd picked something FUNNY—but Derek guessed it SO

QUICKLY!

Unlike me. I took ages to guess what I was...

Am I alive?   Yes.

Am I a singer?   No.

Have I got legs?   Yes.

Am I famous?   No.

Am I Rooster?   No.

Am I an animal?   Kind of.

  (This went on and on and on...)

  Eventually I said,

Am I a bug?

                    Derek just said,

                    YES, close
                    enough.

I'd never have got that. A flea was a good

creature to choose.

weee!

EXTRA snacks
↑ onion ring
Cheese football →

After our game, it was SNACK TIME.

I rummaged through my bag to take out my snack box (again). But I kept finding little **notes** that Mom must have *slipped* into my bag.

Miss you, Tom
xx

Brush your teeth
Mom xx

Mom!

"My mom likes to write me notes," I told Derek. "Did she write this one as well?" Derek asked.

Tom, you have rotten teeth
ha! ha!

"I think Delia did that one."

(Typical.)

136

As I'd eaten most of my snacks already, the only things I had left were the banana biscuits Granny Mavis made and the slightly green bananas.

Norman said he'd eat one if I didn't want them. "Help yourself" I told him before I realized that DELIA had been doodling. (She'd got the banana doodle idea from me. Though Norman didn't seem to mind eating it.)

Delia's handiwork

This seemed like a good time to have a go at drawing something in my journal. It wasn't easy drawing on a moving bus.

Cheese puff

My monster doodles looked a bit wobbly.....

Tₕe bus journey went really ⟹*FAST*, and before we knew it **M**r. Fullerman was announcing,

We're here. Make sure you don't leave anything behind on the bus.

Everyone got more chatty and lively as we turned in to the Activity Center (apart from **M**arcus, who was asleep and drooling).

Mark Clump was about to wake Marcus up when Norman did it for him.

BOO!

As we got off the bus, the Activity Center Team Leaders cheerfully said "HELLO" and showed us the way to the hall.

We took our bags and waited to find out who we'd be sharing the CABINS with.

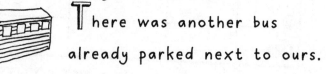

There was another bus already parked next to ours.

But none of us took much notice of it, as we were all too busy looking around.

I told Derek,

The FUN starts HERE!

(Or maybe NOT?)

The team leaders handed out TIDY CABIN FORMS.

(Which didn't look like much fun to me.)

Activity Center
TIDY CABIN FORM

Summer Cabin B

	TIDY	CHECKED	POINTS
DAY 1			
DAY 2			
DAY 3			
DAY 4			

BIG PRIZES FOR THE MOST POINTS!

I'm good at some things—but being tidy isn't one of them.

We were given MAPS of the center too. I've stuck mine here so I don't have to keep

explaining where everything is, which is handy.

I marked my cabin with a STAR on the map.

I was in SUMMER CABIN B, along with: Brad, Norman, Solid, Marcus (I can't get away from him!), Leroy, and Mark.

Derek was in a different cabin with his class—SPRING CABIN B—it was near ours, so not that far away.

You can see on the map there were two more cabins nearby called (you guessed it) AUTUMN and WINTER.

All the cabins had wooden floors and nice comfy bunk beds (brilliant!). Inside the closets there were separate sections for each person sharing a bunk bed, along with a mirror and a few more drawers to stuff things in. Our bags were kept on a rack by the door.

But the only person who could reach the top was Solid (which was handy).

I was going to share with Solid, who really wanted to sleep on the TOP BUNK.

But he got stuck climbing up and changed his mind.

It's too tricky for me,

he told me. Brad Galloway and Norman had already started to run around the room, jumping from bunk to bunk.

Mr. Fullerman stomped into the cabin and pointed to his room with a WARNING.

I don't expect to be disturbed by you messing around all the time, so you'd better BEHAVE, BOYS!

They replied, "Yes, sir."

(But not in a very convincing way.)

Unpacking didn't take me long at all. It's AMAZING what you can stuff into a closet with one hand. "🖐

Solid reminded me that we were supposed to get changed into our sports kit for this afternoon. Which meant taking everything OUT again.

And that's when I found these:

Love U
Tom xx

MORE of Mom's NOTES (groan).

She'd put this one in my sneaker. ↘ MISS You!

I couldn't find my sweatshirt—but I knew it was in there somewhere.
I got distracted when Norman (who was still a bit hyper from all the snacks on the bus) decided to

ROLLLLLLL in a straight line under all the beds while saying...

HELLOoo

It was quite funny right up until he rolled onto Mr. Fullerman's feet.

Get off my feet, Norman, and up off the floor too.

Mr. Fullerman had already told everyone,
"You're only at the Activity Center for THREE DAYS, so it REALLY doesn't matter what bed you choose." (It did to Marcus.)

He had a MASSIVE sulk about what bed he was in. "I won't be able to sleep ZZZZZ if I don't have the end bed," he told Mark Clump (who had the end bed).

Mark Clump said, "OK, I'll swap because I can get a MUCH better view of the

BATS from this bed."

Marcus looked shocked.

What BATS?

Big-foot

"The BATS in the woods over there," Mark said. "They like old trees and sometimes they sleep in barns ... OR maybe even cabins like this one."

Leroy Lewis asked if the BATS would BITE.

"They're not VAMPIRE bats!" Mark assured us.

All this talk about BATS was making Marcus a bit TWITCHY.

"What do you mean,

VAMPIRE BATS?"

"**NO**-not **VAMPIRE BATS**-normal bats. They hang out in corners of rooms or gaps in the ceiling."

Mark Clump told Marcus there was no need to be scared of bats. And Marcus said,

"I'm not scared of BATS-I'm not scared of anything."

(If you say so, Marcus.)

Groan

Then Marcus went and asked **Mr.** Fullerman if he could move beds ~AGAIN!~

He said, "I can't sleep in the corners — I **really** need to be in the middle bed on the <u>TOP</u> bunk."

(I was in the middle bed on the top bunk.)

Mr. Fullerman sighed and told him,

"You don't want to be late for lunch. If Tom doesn't mind moving, that's OK with me."

I was very hungry and just wanted to EAT — so I said, "FINE, I'll move." And I told Marcus I'd get <u>all</u> my stuff later.

Before we left for lunch, I managed to quickly grab my sweatshirt from the floor and followed **Mr.** Fullerman out of the cabin.

On the way to the dining hall, Mr. Fullerman

told us who we were sharing the center with...

GREAT MANOR SCHOOL.

Which made us all groan. That school is SUPER

good at everything.

(Oakfield School vs. Great Manor School

= a WIN for Great Manor School every time.)

Their kids had already:

Neat clothes

Arrived early and changed. Done an activity. Eaten lunch.

Not like us Oakfield School kids—we only

just made it to lunch.

My unpacking

I was standing in the lunch line choosing
what to eat (pasta or chicken—both?)

Ha!
Ha!
Ha!

when I could hear

Ha!
Ha!

LAUGHING coming from behind me.
Derek was already eating—so I chose
the pasta and went to sit down
with him. More people started
laughing, which made me wonder
what was so FUNNY?
Derek and I compared lunches first.
(The same.)
Then cabins. "Any BATS in yours?" I said.
"None that I know of," Derek said.

AMY PORTER and Florence Mitchell
walked past me and THEY
started LAUGHING too.

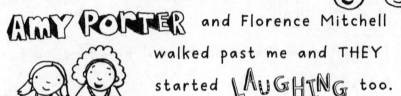

When Marcus joined in I'd had ENOUGH and asked him,

Ha! Ha!   "What's so funny, Marcus?"

He said,

"YOU ARE, TOM!"

Then Derek spotted something STUCK on my back and took it off.

"This might be the reason people

are laughing."

It was ANOTHER one of MOM'S NOTES.

To MY lovely
TOM — MISS
YOU **LOADS**

KISS KISS
from Mom xx

Groan.

(Fingers crossed there are NO
more of Mom's notes anywhere!)

Yuk

FIRST ACTIVITY YEAH!

Team Leader

After lunch,

Team Leader JOE

came to collect us. He wanted to know...

Are you READY to get started?

And we all shouted, "**YES!**"

Then he asked,

"Hands up if you like building and making things?"

I LOVE making stuff, so I got

carried away and shouted,

"YES, ME! I do!"

a bit too loudly.

"Calm down, Tom," Mr. Fullerman said.

(It's Norman who usually gets overexcited.)

155

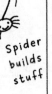

Spider
builds
stuff

Ant
sand-
castle

When Derek was put in the same group as me, I got **EVEN** more excited. (Along with Solid, Norman, Indrani, Marcus, and Julia— who said she was feeling much better now.)

I think Derek and I are pretty good at making things (if I do say so myself).

Last week we made an EXCELLENT den in the garden. It was a **VERY** good place to hang out when:

Yeah!

1. Mom wanted me to clean my room.

2. Delia was looking for her latest copy of **ROCK WEEKLY**.

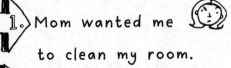

3. Dad kept asking where his biscuits had gone?

Joe and the other team leaders showed us
some STUFF laid out on the grass.

"Can anyone guess what you'll be making today?"

Brad Galloway thought it was funny to

whisper, Cupcakes? He got a BIG

GLARE from MR. Fullerman.

(I laughed.) Mark Clump suggested

we could make a SPACESHIP!

(I could see that sort of working.)

Someone else said, "A house?"

(Maybe, maybe not.)

Then **AMY PORTER** said, (RAFTS?)

Which was the | right ✓ | answer.

Joe told **AMY** "Well done," and explained what he wanted us to do.

1. Think about how to DESIGN our rafts.

2. Work out how to MAKE our rafts.

3. Use the materials provided to BUILD our rafts.

Joe said it was "very important to work together as a team."

(Which was easier said than done with MARCUS in our group.)

He kept suggesting **WEIRD** ways of putting the raft together.

It took us quite a while— but finally, with Team Leader Jenny's help, the raft got (sort of) finished.

start

← Snail race

Mr. Fullerman and the team leaders congratulated us all on

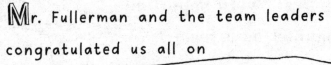

finishing the first activity!

Team Leader Joe said, **"We'll see whose RAFT is going to be the winner in the raft race tomorrow!"**

RAFT RACE — WHAT RAFT RACE?

"I'd forgotten about that," Solid said.

He wasn't the only one.

Building a raft is one thing — RACING it was something else.

"I hope the race is a short one," Derek said.

"I'm not sure our raft will make it."

He had a point.

FINISH

(160)

FIRST night in the CABIN

Norman, Leroy, and Solid wanted to have a midnight **FEAST.**

Which was a brilliant idea.

But I'd eaten most of my treats on the journey (apart from two tattooed bananas).

So at dinnertime I tried to SNEAK out some extra food in my sweatshirt.

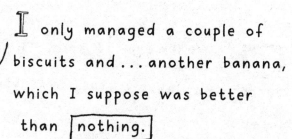

I only managed a couple of biscuits and ... another banana, which I suppose was better than nothing.

On the way to our cabin, we got to chatting with some kids from Great Manor School who seemed nice enough.

They told us about the ^{climbing} **wall** and how
HIGH it was. Marcus Meldrew said,
"That wall doesn't look high to me!"
Even Solid (who's really **TALL**)
thought it looked a bit scary. Marcus boasted,
"I've climbed higher."

"When was that, Marcus?"
Derek asked.
"On holiday—it was a
massive mountain. That wall will be easy
for me to climb," Marcus insisted.

We'll see, I said. Then I reminded
Marcus that all my stuff was still in his
closet.

I really need it back, I said.

Nice biscuits

Dump!!

Marcus just took everything out and dumped it on my bed.

Which would have been OK—if only another one of Mom's notes hadn't fallen out of a sock!

I managed to **grab** it before Marcus read it out **loud** to everyone.

PHEW!

(Mom had gone and mentioned my teddy in the note—which would have been EXTRA embarrassing.)

Brad Galloway suggested that as WELL as a midnight ☾ feast, we should play a few TRICKS on some of the other kids.

What kinds of TRICKS?

Mark Clump wondered.

Hiding stuff in people's beds, that kind of thing.

"What, like an -crumble bed?" Norman said.

I told him, "It's an apple- bed."

"YEAH! We should do one of those." The only problem was, none of us knew how to do an apple-pie bed.

Mr. Fullerman came into the cabin and thought we were all just making our beds neatly.
He said, **"Well done, boys"** and gave us our first POINT on the TIDY CABIN sheet.

 Mark Clump had a̲n̲o̲t̲h̲e̲r̲ idea.
   "Hey, I've got another idea!"
Then he went outside to find a pinecone.

   "What do these remind you of?" he asked us.

   "It's a pinecone, stupid," Marcus said.

   "A mini Christmas tree?" Which was true — they do look like tiny trees—but it wasn't what Mark wanted to hear.

"No—they look like...

MICE."   (Really?)

Mark said, "I'll show you. Just tie a piece of string around the end of the cone, then you pull them along the ground."

 STRING

Leroy still had some string from making the rafts—he gave it to Mark so he could show us. "There, what did I tell you?" (The pinecone still didn't look much like a mouse.) We squinted—and that seemed to help.

Then Mark put the pinecone under his bedcovers and gently pulled the string toward him.

OK—we all got it now.

Norman and Solid made a Sock snake too.

It was perfect timing when a group of kids from Great Manor School walked past our cabin.

Brad SHOUTED, "HEY, LOOK, there's a mouse or some kind of weird CREATURE in our cabin! Come quickly!"

They came to the door and looked around. "Where's this creature, then?" one kid asked. And we all pointed to the bed, where the mouse shape was beginning to move.

Mark Clump
was hiding by
the bed, holding the
string, and began to pull it
toward him.

"What's *THAT?*" one kid said.
"I'm not sure, but it lööks ... suspicious,"
another one said.

(We were all trying not to LAUGH.) Then
one of the little kids said, "I know what we
should do with that kind of creature."

He slowly took off one of his shoes and gave the lump an almighty...

WHACK!

Then another

WHACK!

Until it stopped moving...

completely.

(169)

Gulp

"There, all sorted," he said. "You won't be bothered by that creature anymore."

We all looked SHOCKED. But then the Great Manor kids burst out LAUGHING as they left the cabin.

 Ha! Ha! Ha!

I'm guessing they knew it wasn't a mouse all along. (They did.)

"We're the ones who've been tricked, I think," Solid said.

(We had.)

Broken pinecone

Midnight feasts and tricks

While the team leaders were busy telling everyone to get ready for bed, I was busy searching for my pajamas. Which seemed to be missing.

Luckily **S**olid came to my rescue with an **EXTRA-LARGE** spare T-shirt that came down to my knees. At least I had something to wear now, even if it did look a bit like a nightdress.

Thanks, Solid.

Phew.

Our first night in the cabin started out with **M**r. Fullerman reminding us,

171

"We've got a **PACKED** day tomorrow, so you'll all need a good night's sleep."

(Norman didn't look sleepy at all.)

Mr. Fullerman said, **"Lights out — sleep tight and don't let the bugs bite!"**

"What bugs, sir?" Norman wanted to know.

Mr. Fullerman assured us all that it was just a saying. **"There are no bugs really."** Then he closed the door and turned off the lights.

Mark Clump waited until Mr. Fullerman had 'gone' before he told us,

That's not true, there are LOADS of bugs around.

Norman asked,

In the cabin?

Mark said,

Yes, spiders and that kind of thing are everywhere.

No one wanted to hear that before going to sleep. Mr. Fullerman popped his head around the door again to remind us,

We all said, "Yes, sir." Two minutes later, we all started chatting again.

Oh, and NO midnight feasts or loud snoring either, please!

Norman whispered,

Is it midnight yet?

Which made us laugh.

Ha! Ha! Ha! Ha!

Solid tried to get out of bed quietly, but EVERY floorboard he stepped on CREAKED LIKE CRAZY

when he put his foot down.

Sorry, he whispered. I suggested it would be easier for Solid to stay in his bunk.

We'll come over to you and Marcus.

That way Solid wouldn't wake Mr. Fullerman up. So one by one, we crept over quietly and sneaked out our SNACKS for the midnight feast. * ☾

(Which wasn't at midnight . . .
* ⁂

or much of a **feast** either.)

biscuits

CRISPS

Bread rolls

crisps

CHEWS

CHOC FROG

Choco frog

Granny Mavis would have been proud of
my snacks, though. I had four biscuits and a
banana, so I made biscuit banana sandwiches
and gave one to Solid. (They were a bit
squishy but tasted OK.) →
Norman had a packet of crisps.
He ate them while shining a
flashlight underneath his chin to make scary
faces. Marcus Meldrew said he couldn't
share his sweets because he only had
four sweets left. But I could hear him
in the dark, secretly unwrapping and
eating A LOT more than four sweets.

Sneaky sweets

Then Brad Galloway suddenly remembered that he still had a LARGE bag of **POPCORN**.

He said, "We can share it," which was nice of him.

Norman shone his flashlight on the ground so Brad could get the popcorn.

CREAK

Mr. Fullerman was still moving around in his room. Leroy said, "SHHHHHHHHHhhhhhh" while Brad stood like a statue in case he came back in.

Still

Freeze

Brad waited until it was safe to move. Which took a while. He crept back and tried really hard to open the popcorn. "I can't do it!" he whispered.

Grrrr.

So Solid tried next. Grrrrrrrr.

(It wasn't happening.)

Then Norman and Leroy did their best to open
the popcorn. Which didn't work either, so
I had a go.

It still wouldn't open.

Marcus GRABBED the whole bag from me.

"Give it here, you all are useless. I'll open the
popcorn."

Marcus went and SAT on the

POPCORN.

OOOFFFFF.

Mr. Fullerman came running in and turned on the lights.

"WHAT IS GOING ON?" he said.

(It didn't take long to find out.)

We had to clean up as much popcorn as we could before going back to bed and promising—no more feasts, snacks, or messing around.

"Is that CLEAR, boys?"

"Yes, sir."

After he'd closed the door, we kept quiet for a tiny bit longer than last time.

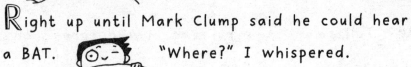

Right up until Mark Clump said he could hear
a BAT. "Where?" I whispered.

"Outside, flying around," Mark said.

"Not a VAMPIRE BAT?" Leroy wanted to know.
We all got up and lOOked out of the window.
I couldn't see any bats.
But we could hear Mr. Fullerman heading
toward the door again. Everyone JUMPED
back into bed as fast as possible.

Then Brad Galloway whispered...

"There's a SNAKE in my bed!"

"Sssshhhhhhhhh,"

we told him.

"It's only our sock snake," Norman said.

Brad LOBBED it over to Norman

and it landed on his bed.

Then Norman chucked it over to Leroy, who said, "Oooffff!" And Leroy threw it back to Norman, who pretended to have a fight with it.

Then Marcus got hold of it and chucked it right at me. Norman told me to chuck it back over to him. I wasn't sure I could throw it that far so I built up a bit of speed by swinging it round and round my head a few times.... Then I finally...let go of the sock snake, which went ...

ks

ZOOMING through the air and landed right on!

Mr. Fullerman's HEAD just as he turned the lights on.
"THIS is your LAST chance unless you want to be doing written work all day tomorrow."

Sorry, sir. (We didn't.)

Morning!

Lovely day!

I thought **M**r. Fullerman would be in a REALLY BAD mood this morning, after our (sort of) midnight feast and sock snake episode. But he was surprisingly JOLLY and very **WIDE-AWAKE.** Not like me.

This was because when everyone else eventually dozed off, **I** discovered that BRAD GALLOWAY "talked" in his sleep. He had a WHOLE conversation with his eyes closed about dogs and how he wanted to take them for a walk.

I tried to wake him up—but nothing worked. He just said,

Wake up, Brad.

> There's a good boy, ready for your WALKIES.

He kept talking all night and didn't remember a thing in the morning.

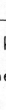

(183)

I hoped Brad wasn't going to do that every night or I might have to swap beds again.

Thanks to Brad's "CHATTING" I was a bit sleepy at breakfast.

Team Leader Jenny shouting, "Morning, everyone!" woke me up a bit. "I hope you all slept well and are ready to have some FUN!"

(Kind of.)

She told us our rafts had been moved to the lake and were ready for the RACE. (GREAT.) "So let's go!"

Team Leader Joe led the way.

We followed them through the woods to the lake, where anyone taking part in the race had to put on a helmet and a life jacket. Marcus insisted on being at the back of the raft.

184

"I can steer it and be in charge," he said.
"Whatever, Marcus," I said (like we had
a choice).

Team Leader Joe reminded everyone,
**"Paddle carefully, as ⟹ straight as you
can, to the finish line. Can everyone do that?"**

We all said, YES (even if we couldn't).

Looking at our raft—I wasn't sure it would
make it that far. Great Manor School was
taking part in the race too, and their rafts
looked a bit different than ours.

Team leader

Julia suggested we should all paddle at the same time (it was a good plan). But Marcus was too busy FLICKing water at Norman and wasn't listening. Then Norman flicked water back, only most of it went onto Mrs. Worthington, who was trying to take photos for the school newsletter.

Stop it!

She shouted, "Stop that, you two!"

When Team Leader Joe BLEW his whistle for the race to start, we all began to paddle like cRAZY—but not at the same time—or in the same direction. Our raft wasn't going very far, mostly just around and around in circles. "PADDLE TOGETHER," Julia told us (again) as we went around for the THIRD TIME.

Marcus stood up (which was a mistake).
"Sit down, Marcus," Derek said, because he was
making the raft WOBBLE.

Eventually we started to move forward
very slowly and WAY behind the other rafts.
I could hear CHEERING at the side of
the lake from the other kids, which kept us
going. Paddling was HARD work.

Just as we got closer to the team
leader holding the finish-line flag,
Marcus managed to DRAG up a
LARGE bit of lake weed with
his paddle, which landed on NORMAN'S
legs. He tried to shake it off,
which made the raft start ROCKING
sideways, backward, and forward.
"STOP moving, it's making me feel sick!" Julia shouted.
Then Marcus STOOD up, which made Norman
lose his balance and topple into the water...

followed by me, Derek, and lastly Julia.

Marcus pretended he didn't know HOW that had happened. We all managed to splash him as we fell in, so he wasn't completely dry. Great Manor School won the race (which was no surprise). And our team came last, but that didn't matter because being in the lake was actually fun (it wasn't very deep).

Our team got out and went back to the cabins to change out of our wet clothes and get ready for an afternoon of wall climbing. Which I hoped would be as much fun as raft racing turned out to be.

WALL CLIMBING

"Yeah!"

As Marcus Meldrew was the only one not to fall in the water — it was even more annoying having to listen to him going ON and ON about how "wall climbing is EASY because I'm VERY brave, you know."

(Really, Marcus ...) So it was a bit of a surprise when at the FIRST SIGHT of the /WALL\, Marcus suddenly developed a VERY bad stomachache.

Which got worse and worse the more he stared UPWARD at the /WALL\.

Norman said he couldn't WAIT to start climbing and wanted to go first.

189

It was AMAZING how *f a s t* he managed to **WHIZZ** up to the top.

"Go, Norman! Go, Norman!" we shouted—which made Marcus groan and hold his stomach even more. Mr. Fullerman decided that Marcus should skip the wall climbing and go to the medical room instead.

(And that seemed to cheer him up.) 😊 When it was my turn, I was a bit slow, but got there in the end (just). Coming back down to the ground turned out to be an adventure too.

Groan.

BUMP!

Everyone, except Marcus, managed to climb the very high /WALL\ .

I would have had a LOT more sympathy for Marcus if I hadn't caught him SCOFFING LOADS MORE SWEETS when we got *huh?* back to the cabin.

He said the *sweets* had made him feel better AND ... he could definitely climb that wall now. (No problem.) (Knowing full well it was too late.)

Solid told Marcus, "Climbing the wall was a LOT harder than it looked." After hiding his sweets, Marcus said, "It didn't look that hard to me."

"How would YOU know?" I wondered. And Marcus said, "It wasn't my fault I got a stomachache. I'm a good climber and BRAVE too."

"You're **not THAT** brave," I said, which was <u>true</u>.

"Well, you're not either," Marcus said.

"How do you work that one out?" I asked him.

"A BRAVE person wouldn't need to bring a cuddly-wuddly teddy bear to bed with them."

HUH?

Marcus had been snooping.

"Thanks a lot, Marcus," I said, feeling a bit embarrassed.

Roar!

Then Brad said, "What's wrong with having a teddy bear?" Turns out I wasn't the only person hiding a soft toy after all.

"I can't sleep without mine," Leroy said.

Which **SHUT** Marcus up.

Though if I was **N**orman, I might have kept
quiet about having a

SNUGGLE BLANKET.

"Doesn't anyone else have a snuggle
blanket, then?"

No, just you, Norman.
(It looked a bit manky too.)

DINNER-TIME

Here's a picture of my ``empty'' plate because I **SCOFFED** [all] my dinner tonight as it was the BEST! AND I had seconds of ice cream too.

Tiny chip
crumbs
left

Marcus couldn't finish his after all the secret sweets he ate earlier. — Yuk

Team Leader Jenny told us we had a little something else to look forward to now as well.

Then she handed everyone a small package or envelope to open.

I got [two] letters and some caramel wafers. Even though we're not away for THAT long, it was nice to get a letter and TREATS! 🖼

(I'm guessing the teachers brought everything with them—so we all got our letters at the same time.) Here's mine: 🔽

Hello, Tom!

We hope you're having a GREAT time doing lots of EXCITING activities at the center.
    The house is very quiet without you. But while you've been away we'll be busy painting your bedroom (it will look great when you get home!) and making it MUCH neater too. Which won't be difficult.
    Here are a few wafers for the journey home. Don't eat them now.
    We'll see you very soon.
    Much love,
    Mom and Dad xx

Then I got a **surprise**, as the other letter was from ... Delia.

Tom,

I wish I could say I was missing you but that would be a lie.

While you're away Dad's going to paint and decorate your bedroom. He couldn't decide what color to do it. So I suggested a mixture of stripes and spots might be nice...in different colors.

When you get back, you might need a pair of my sunglasses to look at it.

Granny Mavis is making you a WELCOME HOME CAKE. I hope you like cabbage.

I told her it was your favorite so it will be in the cake.

(Ha! Ha!) From Delia x

Then I noticed there was a P.S. on another page.

P.S. I found your DUDE3 design-a-T-shirt competition entry. You forgot to MAIL it, numbskull.

P.P.S. It wasn't bad either.

NO WAY!

I'd worked SO hard on that design too. I can't believe I forgot to mail it.

Marcus offered me a sweet, I looked so fed up.

"No, thanks," I said.

(I hardly EVER say no to sweets.)

Want a sweet?

Groan.

Owl Trouble

Summer Cabin B (that's us) had been RUBBISH at getting points on the TIDY ROOM chart. We all kept forgetting to make our beds and that kind of thing. Derek told me that his cabin (Spring B) was trying to be EXTRA neat because apparently there's a MASSIVE PRIZE for the tidiest cabin at the end of the trip. There is?

He says that Mrs. Nap's in charge of the prize "so who knows what it will be."

First prize

Abacus

Speaking of PRIZES, I showed Derek the letter from Delia. He read the first part and said,

"I'm so glad I don't have a sister."

"It gets worse. Read the last page," I told him. Derek shook his head. "Oh, no! How did you forget to mail your T-shirt competition design?"

 "Who knows, I just forgot," I said.

(I think this might have been why.)

T-shirt design hidden

MESS

Derek was gutted for me. He thought I might have won too. "You never know, there might be another competition you can enter," Derek said, trying to be all cheerful for me.

"Yeah, maybe."

(I'm pretending to be OK, but inside I'm doing this...)

AGH!

199

Getting back to the (very messy) cabin — Solid
thought it would be funny to hide
in the closet (which was a bit of a squeeze),
then ═══ *LEAP* out at whoever opened
the door.

Which in this case...was ME.

SURPRISE!

I got a bit of a

SHOCK,

but at least it took my mind off NOT
mailing my T-shirt competition design for a bit.
Norman said he wanted to be a bat
and sleep up^side down tonight.
He told everyone,   "It's quite comfy."

(It didn't look comfy to me.)
Norman changed his mind
when his face went all
RED.
I told him, "Your face is
as red as Mr. Keen's when he's angry."

When **M**r. Fullerman came in to tell us
about tonight's campfire treat, he did a quick
head count to check we were all in the cabin.

Where's Solid?

We pointed to the closet, where he was hiding
again. **M**r. Fullerman opened the door and
SOLID *LEAPED* out at him, SHOUTING,

We all thought it
was funny (even if
Mr. Fullerman didn't).

11

I'm writing this by flashlight because BRAD is TALKING in his SLEEP AGAIN! Which is beginning to freak me out a bit.

He's mumbling something about MARSHMALLOWS....

I think he's reliving the campfire treats we had tonight.

That's what it sounds like.

It was a FUN evening, which started out nicely enough.

Mmmm, yummy hot chocolate.

zzzzzzz

Here's what happened...

202

Our team leaders organized a wonderful campfire for us to sit around. AND they gave us hot chocolate and toasted marshmallows too.

The teachers were all very pleased with the way the trip was going.

Phew

Relief. Nearly done. They said everything seemed to be working out well. No accidents (knock on wood, Mr. Fullerman), no one was too homesick or sick (Marcus's stomachache didn't count).

We were all having a great time (with just one more day to go).

Mrs. Worthington told everyone not to get too close to the campfire. "You don't want anything to **SINGE** from the heat."

"Like a mustache," 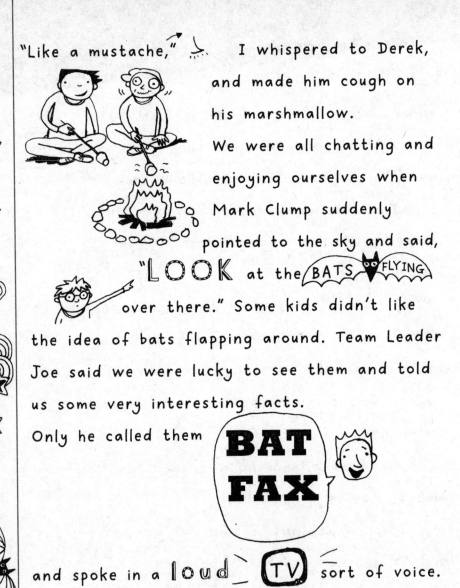 I whispered to Derek, and made him cough on his marshmallow.

We were all chatting and enjoying ourselves when Mark Clump suddenly pointed to the sky and said, "LOOK at the BATS FLYING over there." Some kids didn't like the idea of bats flapping around. Team Leader Joe said we were lucky to see them and told us some very interesting facts.

Only he called them BAT FAX

and spoke in a loud TV sort of voice.

BAT FAX ONE: BATS aren't actually blind; they can 👁 👁 see perfectly well. So the saying "Blind as a bat" is rubbish, really.

BAT FAX TWO: A single bat can eat over six hundred bugs in an hour — which is a bit like a person eating <u>twenty</u> pizzas a day!

BAT FAX THREE: A baby bat is called a PUP.

(I'm a pup.)

(That's a good one — I'll tell my dad that one.)

Then Team Leader Alan cleared his throat and asked us if we'd like to hear a special campfire song?   (Why not?)

"You can all join in." Alan brought out his guitar and was about to start singing.

When he opened his mouth, this noise came
out ...

TWERRRWITTT
TERRWHOOOO

(Which wasn't what we expected.)

Julia Morton shouted,

"WHAT WAS THAT?"

AMY said it sounded like an owl.

TWERRRWITTT
TEERRWHOOOO

There it was again.

Joe said, "That sounds very much like a tawny owl in the trees. Who wants to take a look?"

Everyone did.

Mr. Fullerman got the MOST excited.

He whispered to us all,

"Look how CLOSE it is."

(It was quite close.)

We crept up as quietly as we could. Joe pointed to the owl that was sitting in the tree looking at us. Mr. Fullerman said,

"That's AMAZING. Look at its feathers and those eyes. I don't think I've ever seen such big eyes on an owl before, have you?"

I whispered to Derek, "Are you thinking what I'm thinking?"

Yes, he was.

Teacher   Owl

It had been a very long day—and all that owl watching had made it even longer.

Back in the cabin, I was STILL listening to Brad SLEEP TALKING

(groan)

when I finally thought of a good way to wake him up without getting out of my bunk.

Chat chat chat

I would do my impression of an OWL hooting.

TTTERRWITT
TERRWOOO!
TTTTERRRWITTT
TERRRRWOOOO!

It was SUCH a good OWL hoot that everyone else in the cabin woke up ... apart from Brad.

TTTERRWITT   TERRWOOO!

Mr. Fullerman woke up too and thought the owl was BACK. I pretended the noise came from OUTSIDE. "It's that OWL again ... it woke ME up too!" I told everyone.

Mr. Fullerman said he would go outside and SHOO the owl away.

He told us, **"Now go back to sleep, all of you."**

Yes, sir.

I'm back!

Norman and Solid's sock snake
started being thrown around the cabin again.

Only this time when it came to me,
I found A MUCH BETTER use for it that
managed to wake ☉☉ Brad up.

And I got some sleep...

Wake up,
Brad.

eventually.

In the morning the last person to wake up was Marcus. Looking at him *snoozing* with his mouth open, I had what I thought was an excellent idea.

I got my teddy and the other cuddly toys from Brad and Leroy. We made them all cozy right next to him.

Marcus stayed like that right up until Norman added his SNUGGLE BLANKET. (I think the WHIFF of it woke him up.) I took a good photo to stick in my journal, though....

Today was our **LAST** day of doing activities. (Derek said it was kayaking—which is sort of like canoeing?)

We'd all be going home in the afternoon and I was (a tiny bit) sad.

WHOOP!

Yeah!

You're off!

Mind you, the team leaders didn't Seem that upset. From the way they were being all **EXTRA KEEN** and **JOLLY**, you'd almost think they were pleased to see us leave.

Before we were allowed to kayak on the lake, the team leaders brought us to the swimming pool and showed us some important safety stuff, along with reassuring some kids that "there are no sharks or **MONSTERS** in the lake." The Great Manor kids were already there

and making everything look easy
(it wasn't).

Once we got in the kayaks, Marcus said
I kept getting in his way.

But he was the one wobbling all over the
place. It took me a while to learn how to turn
my kayak around and paddle in a straight line.
Team Leader Jenny eventually told me,
"Well done, Tom, that was
ABSOLUTELY FANTASTIC.
You're ready to kayak on the lake."
Which was good news... and right in front of
Marcus too — he looked pleased for me.

The lake was A LOT murkier than I
remembered it, with ducks, birds, and leaves
all floating around.

Marcus had to wait his turn and wasn't happy. I paddled to the other side of the lake and right back to the shallow end. Marcus was shou**ting** at me to **HURRY UP!** So I decided to go around one more time.

I carefully turned the kayak around and was about to set off again when it got STUCK.

The more I paddled, the less I moved (which was annoying).

It was only when Team Leader Joe told Marcus to

"STOP HOLDING TOM'S KAYAK!"

that I realized what he was doing!

STUCK

When Marcus let go ...
I SHOT off

like a ROCKET...

which took Marcus by surprise.
He lost his balanc and landed in the lake right
next to the ducks—who looked even

more SHOCKED than

he was.

huh

At least Mrs. Worthington was there to
take a few ACTION pictures for the school
newsletter.

There were going to
be some good ones
to choose from.

I won!

1st place

After the EXCELLENT kayaking, Mrs. Nap told us that some Great Manor School kids had come first in the Tidy Cabin AWARD (which wasn't really a surprise).

The REAL SHOCK was finding out they'd won a MASSIVE bar of

chocolate.

"If I'd known that was the prize, I would have at least tried not to be so messy," I told Solid as we walked back to the cabin to get ready to leave.

I managed to pack my bag the same way I unpacked it (which didn't take long). It was a bit heavier on the way home, with a few more soggy towels and T-shirts.

STUFF

Norman suggested we should all sit at the back of the bus this time.

"It's more fun." So we got a move on and tried to SNAG the back seats.

Mrs. Nap and the team leaders had gone around all the cabins to do one LAST check before we left.

On the bus, the whole group did a

"Three cheers for the TEAM LEADERS and the TEACHERS!

Hip hip hooray!"

Then Mrs. Nap held up some of the stuff she'd found.

"Whose cat-shaped toothbrush?"

It's Julia's.

"Someone's FLUFFY bed socks?"

 Norman said they were his.

Then she held up a smelly-looking T-shirt

and a nasty sweatshirt. (No one claimed them.)

"And last but not least—who's this lovely

 teddy belong to, then?"

Some kids went "Arrrrrhhhhh!"

Derek nudged me and said,

"That's yours, Tom?" (Oh, no ... so it was.)

 I mumbled and slowly put up

my hand. "It's mine."

"Who said that?"

218

"Me, Mrs. Nap..."

"Is that TOM? Is this YOUR TEDDY
                        BEAR, TOM?"

 "Yes." Groan.

I didn't think it was possible to make me feel
any more embarrassed about my teddy.
Then she did this...
Mrs. Nap made MY teddy
wave at everyone as she
walked all the way down the bus,   WAVE

   RIGHT to the very back where I was sitting.
 Thanks, Mrs. Nap.

(Maybe sitting at the back of the bus
            wasn't such a good idea after all.)
            At least I got to use him as a
            pillow for the rest of the journey.

(219)

Journey home

On the way back, someone spotted Great Manor School's bus, which had stopped at the side of the road. We waved as we went past and noticed that some of the kids didn't look too well.

Mr. Fullerman said, **"Oh, dear — looks like they ate too much of that prize-winning chocolate bar."**

Tidy cabin + chocolate + bus = yuck.

I told Derek it wouldn't have made ME sick if we'd won it.

As we got closer to home, everybody was starting to get a little bit excited.

I wasn't sure who was coming to pick me up. Either Mom or Dad or maybe both?

But definitely NOT Delia.

GO AWAY.

The bus had to drive past the school first,
then turn around to pull up on the right side
of the sidewalk.

It gave us all a good chance to see who
was waiting for us. Derek spotted
Rooster first, then his dad.
I couldn't see anyone yet.

When we got off the bus, Rooster was
pleased to see Derek,
I could tell.

I told Mr. Fingle that I didn't
need a lift, as my mom and dad were coming
to pick me up.

Derek said, "BAND PRACTICE this Sunday?"
as he left. Which was a good idea.

(I'll write that on the *calendar* when I get home.)

There was no sign of Mom or Dad at all. One by one all the kids, friends, parents, and families disappeared, and I was the only one left.

Mr. Fullerman said, **"I'll give your mom and dad a call. Bring your bag and come into school to wait. I'm sure there's a good reason why they're late."** (I hope so.)

Mrs. Mumble was in the school office, and so was Mr. Keen. Mr. Keen asked if I'd had a good time?

"Yes, sir, I did have a great time, right up until now."

Mr. Fullerman reappeared and said that someone was coming to collect me **"right away. They'll be here in five minutes. They thought you were due back tomorrow."** (Great.)

I had to sit in the STAFF room (awkwardly holding my teddy) waiting to be picked up.

I kept looking out of the window for our car to pull up with Mom and Dad in it. SO it was a BIG SURPRISE when I suddenly caught sight of...

THE FOSSILS.

Yeah! Tom!

Welcome home, Tom!

Going FULL *SPEED* toward the school with their mobility scooter.

(It wasn't that fast — just speedy for them.) They waved at me from the school grounds.

I told Mr. Fullerman, "My grandparents are here." So he took me downstairs to meet up with them.

Mom and Dad were shopping,

Well? Looks great. Sigh.

Granddad told me.

New hat

"Your mom said that SOMEONE wrote the wrong day on the *calendar*. We all thought you were due home tomorrow," Granny Mavis said.

It was nice of **THE FOSSILS** to come and pick me up. But they really [didn't] need to bring the flags. ((Welcome home, Tom!)) (I'm glad they were late and no one else was here to see them now.)

It took me a bit longer to get home walking next to the mobility scooter.

Granny Mavis reminded me that Dad had been painting and decorating my room while I was away. I'd FORGOTTEN about that!

"It looks different," Granddad added, which was a bit of a worry.

"Different" is something I'd say when I couldn't think of anything else.

So when I got home, I went straight to my room to see what "different" really meant.

Apart from the bit DELIA had messed

with . . .

My room looked AMAZING and so much tidier too. It was freshly painted white, and on one wall, Dad had painted my very OWN special BLACKBOARD doodle wall.

← Chalk

How good was that?

Mom and Dad weren't back yet, so I got rid of Delia's "Welcome home" message and decided to draw a few of my favorite moments from my trip to show them when they got home.

There were lots to choose from.

GO AWAY TOM

Ha! Ha!

It was a great trip, but it's nice to be home!

Ha! Ha!

I still have some bandages left—which are very good for sticking on the back of my journal.

Three days can feel like a long time to be AWAY (even though I know it's not).

It's great to get back to doing some of the things that I haven't been able to do for a while, like:

* Playing with Rooster.

* Having the bathroom to myself. (Delia hasn't been around much, which is also good.)

* Being back in my own bed, sleeping peacefully without being woken up by BATS or chatting. (I don't miss that at all.)

A few other things happened when I was away.

Mom managed to find out exactly WHEN the cousins were coming to stay after all.

And it's THIS weekend.

(She had to take a sneaky peek at Auntie Alice's calendar to find out.)

Aha!

I write everything in.

AND THIS sign went up next door, which has sent Mom into EXTRA NOSY mode. She's desperate to find out who's moving in. She says, "I hope we find out soon."

SOLD

(I just HOPE it's not that annoying girl with the faces.)

D ad says when the cousins come over we might go out to eat for a change....

"As a special treat." (YEAH!)

"There's a new place in town that's just opened up, which would be good for the cousins too," he adds.

"Why would it be good for the cousins?" I ask.

"It's an all-you-can-eat place."

Sounds like my kind of restaurant.

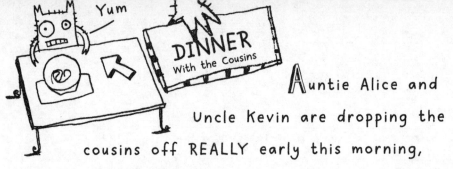

Yum

DINNER
With the Cousins

Auntie Alice and Uncle Kevin are dropping the cousins off REALLY early this morning, so Mom and Dad are rushing around cleaning the house.

I'm trying to watch some TV before they arrive, but Mom keeps puffing up cushions and vacuuming around me, which is annoying.

When they all arrive, Auntie Alice tells Mom, "The house looks SO tidy, I hope you didn't clean especially for us!"

And Mom says, "NO, of course not, we always clean on the weekends."

(Which is news to me.)

I take the cousins and show them my new doodle wall. They like it a LOT. "Here, you can draw if you want," I say.

"What shall we draw?" they ask.

So I suggest they could draw a **MONSTER** or maybe some funny pictures of their family. "I do it all the time."

Their doodles don't go down too well with Auntie Alice or Uncle Kevin when they come up to say goodbye. As they're leaving, Dad tells Uncle Kevin, "You have to admit, it was a good likeness, Kevin."

(It was.)

I ask the cousins if they fancy a snack?
(Like I don't know the answer already.) ☺

　　We go down to the kitchen to see what
there is to eat. "Oh, look," I say, pretending to
be surprised. "We have bananas ...
lots of them. Help yourselves."

Luckily for me, they do,
which helps the numbers go down.

　　　　I'm getting a bit fed up with
　　　　bananas.
　　　　Dad's asking them about school
and what are they up to and even worse,
"What kind of music do you like,
then, boys?" Which is embarrassing,
especially as he's never heard of
ANYONE they say.

Worse still, Mom wants to know if we want
to make biscuits?　　BISCUITS!

"**M**OM! They won't want to make biscuits.... You don't, do you?"

 "Why not?" they say. "We like making biscuits." (That's a surprise to me.)

Mom gets out all the ingredients and we make biscuits. We make a bit of a mess too, but I get away with leaving it because the cousins are here.

Delia has suddenly appeared and is hovering around, trying to help herself to one of our freshly cooked biscuits. So I tell her,

"If you want a biscuit, you need to SAY, '**Please** may I have a biscuit, my lovely brother, **Tom**?' and I might let you have one."

The rest of the day I keep the cousins busy by watching (non-scary) films.

We go next door and hang out with Derek

while taking Rooster for a walk. Which is fun.

Derek says, "Your cousins are very tall, aren't they."

"Do you think so?" I say as we walk behind them.

GOING OUT

We're getting ready to go out to eat when Dad does his usual thing of rushing around the house unplugging all the appliances. We're all sitting in the car waiting to go when he remembers one he's missed. Mom says, "Come ON, Frank, we'll be late!"

I want him to hurry up because I'm a bit squashed in the car.

When we get to the restaurant, it's REALLY busy, with loads of families all piling their plates up with food. We're shown to a table and told that depending on what size plate we have, that's how much it costs to eat.

ALL YOU CAN EAT

Dad says we can all have a MEDIUM-size plate. "That's more than enough, I think."

small medium large

⃝ ⃝ ◯   There's SO much food to choose from I don't know where to start!

The cousins seem to know what to do.

pasta

I can't help thinking I've been here before, even though I know I haven't.
I go and help myself to a really nice dinner of everything I love.

Mom tries to add some extra vegetables to my plate, which makes some of my food spill over onto the table. She says,   whoops.
"Never mind ... whoops!

groan

waitress

"I'll ask the waitress to clear it up."

But the waitress we've got doesn't
want to come over.

She even turns her back on Mom and tries
to ignore her. Mom has to find someone else
to help instead.

Mom says, "CHARMING. I'm not
leaving a tip for her!"

Dad's plate isn't too bad. He reminds Mom
about his body being a temple again, which
makes both of us roll our eyes.

But the cousins' plates are something else.

They spend AGES stacking them up as carefully as they can, with as much food as possible. They're balanced like a tall tower. If someone hadn't accidentally knocked into them, they would have made it to the table, too.

But they didn't.

AGH!
We watched
TWO huge
mountains of food
collapse over the floor and
tables and splatter
some of the other
diners too. Who
weren't very happy.

The entire restaurant
was staring at the food and us. It was REALLY
embarrassing. Especially for one waitress who
was sent over to help clean up the mess....

At least we all know where Delia works
n**O**w. And where I'd seen those hats before!
(Mom decided to leave her a tip after all.)

When Delia got home later I told her
the food was very nice just before she
SLAMMED her bedroom door.

In the morning she was still **MAD**.

"This WHOLE family is a NIGHTMARE. And you WONDER WHY I didn't want to tell you where I worked!"

She's got a point. It was quite funny, though. The cousins don't help much by reliving the whole story for Auntie Alice when she comes to pick them up. She says they had a nice weekend but Uncle Kevin's golf swing was a bit crooked so he's recovering at home with a cricked neck.

← sore neck

When I got home from school today,
THIS letter was waiting for me.

For the attention of:
Tom Gates
24 Castle Road
UK

ROCK WEEKLY

Not just any old letter – it's from
ROCK WEEKLY magazine.

I know this is going to sound really WEIRD,
but I take back EVERYTHING I've ever said
that was BAD about having a grumpy sister.

I can honestly say that RIGHT now (it might change later) my sister DELIA is the best sister in the whole wide world EVER. I actually want to go and HUG her and say thank you — thank you — thank you — to her for being so brilliant and

ABSOLuTELY FANTASTIC
(at most things).

Because the letter from **ROCK WEEKLY** magazine says that I've gone and WON the T-shirt design competition!
So NOW **DUDE3** will be printing and WEARING my design. I get some FREE T-shirts too.
I am so EXCITED I can hardly breathe.
I've been leaping around the room and have already run over to tell Derek, who's just as excited as I am.

So the REASON I have to be nice to Delia
               (for as long as I possibly can)
is because she found my design that I
completely forgot to mail and mailed it for me.
My entry got there in time for the deadline.

I'm SO HAPPY!

Delia is a little uncomfortable with me
being so nice to her.
"It feels odd. Back off, will you?" she tells me
when I bring her a cup of tea.

The only thing Delia really wants from me is:

1. I (or any family member) am not allowed
   to come to THAT restaurant again when
   she's there. (Fine by me.)

2. One of my T-shirts when I get them. (No problem.)
3. To stay out of her room. (OK, will do.)
4. To stop writing stupid songs about her. (Even though they're not stupid.)

What have you put in it?

Mom and Dad say how nice it is to see us getting along so well.

And Delia says, "Don't worry, it won't last."

(Which is probably true.)

The end.

How to do a BANANA doodle

→ Take a banana and a toothpick
　　　　　(mind the sharp ends).

Carefully push the stick into the banana skin—not too deep.

Where you make a hole it will turn black.
You can do a doodle like this quite quickly.

Don't leave the banana too long before you eat it, as the doodle will go darker and darker (then go moldy—yuck).

Did you find all the monsters?

I am ABSOLUTELY Fantastic
(at SOME things).

LIKE drawing MONSTERS

monster
slime

BUT I am NOT so good at drawing
REAL hands
or feet (which are tricky).
Here's a picture of Marcus with
MONSTER hands and duck feet instead.

I'd forgotten about the new neighbors until . . .

(To be continued . . .)

Tom Gates' Glossary

(Which means explanations for stuff
that might sound a bit ODD.)

Yum!

⟵ Biscuits ≅ cookies.

Caramel wafers: Excellent biscuits (cookies)

⬆ covered in

chocolate with layers of

caramel and wafer inside. ⟹

Crisps: Chips.

 ⟵ Garden is a YARD.

MANKY means

disgusting or revolting.

For instance, this mint

that rolled on the

floor is manky.

◄ (So is Rooster's fur.)

Rubbish

Garbage

Mate = Friend.

School Activity Trip ≅ Class Trip.

Sports
Kit

Gym
Clothes

Tea towels ≅ dish towels.

When Liz was little, she loved to draw, paint, and make things. Her mom used to say she was very good at making a mess (which is still true today!).

She kept drawing and went to art school, where she earned a degree in graphic design. She worked as a designer and art director in the music industry, and her freelance work has appeared on a wide variety of products.

Liz is the author-illustrator of several picture books. Tom Gates is the first series of books she has written and illustrated for older children. They have won several prestigious awards, including the Roald Dahl Funny Prize, the Waterstones Children's Book Prize, and the Blue Peter Book Award. The books have been translated into forty-three languages worldwide. Liz works in a nice cozy shed in her yard and lives in (mostly) sunny Brighton, England with her husband and three (not so little anymore) children. She doesn't have a pet but she does have lots of squirrels in the yard that eat everything in sight (including her tulip bulbs, which is annoying).